RHYMING LIFE & DEATH

Books by Amos Oz

Fiction

Nonfiction

For Children

RHYMING
LIFE & DEATH

—

Amos Oz

Translated from the Hebrew by
Nicholas de Lange

Houghton Mifflin Harcourt
BOSTON • NEW YORK
2009

For information about permission to reproduce
selections from this book, write to Permissions,
Houghton Mifflin Harcourt Publishing Company,
6277 Sea Harbor Drive, Orlando, Florida 32887-6777.

www.hmhbooks.com

Library of Congress Cataloging-in-Publication Data
Oz, Amos.
[Haruze ha-hayim veha-mavet. English]
Rhyming life and death / Amos Oz ; translated from
the Hebrew by Nicholas de Lange.
p.   cm.
ISBN 978-0-15-101367-8
I. De Lange, N. R. M. (Nicholas Robert Michael),
date. II. Title.
PJ5054.O9H3713 2009
892.4'36—dc22   2008049207

Book design by Melissa Lotfy
Text is set in Whitman.

Printed in the United States of America

DOC 10 9 8 7 6 5 4 3 2 1

RHYMING LIFE & DEATH

THESE ARE THE MOST COMMONLY ASKED QUESTIONS. Why do you write? Why do you write the way you do? Are you trying to influence your readers, and, if so, how? What role do your books play? Do you constantly cross out and correct or do you write straight out of your head? What is it like to be a famous writer and what effect does it have on your family? Why do you mostly describe the negative side of things? What do you think of other writers: which ones have influenced you and which ones can't you stand? And by the way, how would you define yourself? How would you respond to those who attack you, and what do the attacks do to you? Do you write with a pen or on a computer? And how much, roughly, do you earn from each book? Do you draw the material for your stories from your imagination or directly from life? What does your ex-wife think of the female characters in your books? And, in fact, why did you leave your first wife, and your second wife?

1

Do you have fixed times for writing or do you just write when the muse visits you? Are you politically committed as a writer, and, if so, what is your political affiliation? Are your books autobiographical or completely fictional? And above all, how is it that, as a creative artist, you lead such a stolid, unexciting private life? Or are there all sorts of things that we don't know about you? And how can a writer, an artist, spend his life working as an accountant? Or is it simply a job for you? And tell us, doesn't being an accountant totally kill your muse? Or do you have another life, one that's not for publication? Won't you at least give us a few hints this evening? And would you please tell us, briefly and in your own words, what exactly you were trying to say in your last book?

There are clever answers and there are evasive answers: there are no simple, straightforward answers.

And so the Author will sit down in a little café three or four streets away from the Shunia Shor Community Center building where the literary evening is to take place. The interior of the café feels low, gloomy, and suffocating, which is why it suits him rather well right now. He will sit here and try to concentrate on these questions. (He always arrives half an hour or forty minutes early for any meeting, and so he always has to find something to do to pass the time.) A tired waitress in a short skirt, and with high breasts, dabs a cloth over his table: but the Formica remains sticky even after she has wiped it. Maybe the cloth was not clean?

While she does it the Author eyes her legs: they are shapely, attractive legs, although the ankles are a little on the thick side. Then he steals a look at her face: it is a pleasant, sunny face, with eyebrows that meet in the middle and the hair tied back with a red rubber band. The Author detects a smell of sweat and soap, the smell of a weary woman. He can make out the outline of her underpants through her skirt. His eyes fix on this barely discernible shape: he finds a slight asymmetry in favor of the left buttock exciting. She notices his look groping at her legs, her hips, her waist, and her face expresses disgust and entreaty: just leave me alone, for heaven's sake.

And so the Author politely looks away, orders an omelet and salad with a roll and a glass of coffee, extracts a cigarette from its packet, and holds it unlit in between the second and third fingers of his left hand which is supporting his cheek: an intensely cultured look that fails to impress the waitress because she has already turned on the heels of her flat shoes and vanished behind the partition.

While he waits for his omelet, the Author imagines the waitress's first love (he decides to name the waitress Ricky): when Ricky was only sixteen she fell in love with the reserve goalkeeper of Bnei-Yehuda football team, Charlie, who turned up one rainy day in his Lancia in front of the beauty parlor where she worked and swept her away for a three-day break in a hotel in Eilat (of which an uncle of his was part-owner). While they were there, he even bought her a sensational evening dress with silver sequins and everything, that made her look like a Greek singer, but after two weeks or so he dropped her and went off again to the same hotel, this time with the runner-up in the Queen of the Waves contest. Eight years and four men later, Ricky has never stopped dreaming that one day he will come back: he had episodes where he would seem to be terribly angry with her, really scary, dangerous, as if he was about to go crazy, and she was quite alarmed at times, but suddenly, in an instant, his mood would lighten and he would forgive her, cuddling her with childlike happiness, calling her Gogog, kissing her neck, tickling her with his warm breath, gently parting her lips with his nose, like this, which gave her a warm sensation that crept over her body, like honey, then suddenly he would toss her up in the air, hard, like a pillow, until she screamed for her mother, but he always caught her at the very last moment and hugged her, so she wouldn't fall. He liked to tickle her with the tip of his tongue, slowly for a long time behind both ears and inside her ears and on the nape of her neck where the finest hairs grew, until that feeling crept over her like honey again. Charlie never raised a finger against her or called her names. He was the first man who taught her to slow-dance, and to wear a micro bikini, and to lie naked face down in the sun and think dirty thoughts, and he was the first man to teach her what drop earrings with green stones did for her face and neck.

But then he was forced to return the Lancia and wear a plaster cast on his fractured arm and he went off to Eilat again but this time with a different girl, Lucy, who almost won the Queen of the Waves competition, and, before he left, he said to Ricky, Look here, Gogog, I'm really really sorry but try to understand. Lucy was before you, Lucy and I didn't really break up, we just had a bit of a spat and somehow it turned out that we didn't see each other for a while, but now we're back together again and that's that, Lucy said to tell you that she's really not mad at you, no hard feelings, you'll see, Gogog, after a while you'll gradually get over our thing together and I'm sure you'll find someone who suits you more, because the fact is, you deserve someone better, you deserve the best there is. And the most important thing, Gogog, is that you and I only have good feelings about each other, no?

Eventually Ricky gave the sequined dress away to a cousin and relegated the bikini to the back of a drawer, behind her sewing kit, where it was forgotten: men can't help themselves, that's just the way they are made, but women in her view are actually not much better, and that's why love is something that one way or another always turns out badly.

Charlie hasn't played for Bnei-Yehuda for a long while. Now he has a wife and three children and owns a factory in Holon making solar water heaters — they say he even exports them wholesale to the Occupied Territories and to Cyprus. And what about that Lucy? With her skinny legs? What happened to her in the end? Did Charlie throw her away too when he'd finished using her? If only I had her address, or her phone number, and if I had the guts, I'd go and look her up. We could have a coffee together. And talk. We might even become friends, the two of us. It's strange how I don't give a damn about him anymore but I do care a bit about her. I never think about him at all, even with contempt, while I do sometimes think about her: because maybe she's become a bit like me now? Did he call her Gogog in bed, too? Did he laugh and move the tip of his nose back and forth like that between her lips? Did he show her, slowly, gently, with her hand, what her body was like? If only I could find her, we might talk about that, we might even become friends.

Friendship is something that doesn't enter into relations between a man and a woman, especially if there's electricity there. And if there's no electricity then there can't be anything between them anyway. But between two women, especially two women who've both been on the receiving end of suffering and disappointment from men, and above all two women who've both suffered on account of the same man — maybe I should try to find that Lucy sometime?

At a nearby table two men are sitting, both in their fifties. They seem unhurried. The dominant one is thickset and totally bald, and looks like a gangster's henchman in a film. The smaller of the two looks used, even threadbare, his manner is noisy, his expression inclined to show admiration or sympathy, without discrimination. The Author, lighting a cigarette, decides that this one must be an agent of sorts, or perhaps a hairdryer salesman. He names the boss Mr. Leon, and the toady could be Shlomo Hougi. They seem to be having a general discussion on the subject of success.

The gangster's henchman is saying, "Besides which, by the time you've made anything of your life it's over."

"I agree one hundred percent," says the sidekick, "God forbid I should contradict you, but surely you must agree that living just to eat and drink can hardly be considered a life worthy of a human being. A man needs to have a degree of spirituality, as we call it in Judaism, an 'extra soul.'"

"There you go, again," says the boss, coldly and with a hint of disgust, "always taking off on one of your woolly ramblings. You're always pulling things out of thin air. You'd explain yourself much better if you just gave an example or two from real life."

"OK, fine, why not, take for instance that guy Hazzam who used to work for Isratex, Ovadya Hazzam, you remember him, don't you, the one who won half a million on the lottery a couple of years ago, and then he got divorced, had a wild time, moved house, started investing, offered unsecured loans to all and sundry, joined the party and maneuvered to become head of department, and lived like a king. Like a lord, even. In the end he got liver cancer and was taken to Ichilov Hospital in critical condition."

Mr. Leon screws up his face and says in a bored tone: "Of course. Ovadya Hazzam. I was at his son's wedding. As it happens I am personally acquainted with the case of Ovadya Hazzam. He spent money left and right, both on good causes and just having a good time, he cruised around town all day in a blue Buick with Russian blondes, and he was always looking for investors, entrepreneurs, guarantors, sources of funding, partners. Poor guy. But you know what? For what we were talking about, you'd best forget him: he's not a good example for you. Cancer, my friend, doesn't come from bad habits. Scientists have discovered now that it's caused either by dirt or by nerves."

The Author leaves nearly half his omelet on his plate. He takes a couple of sips of his coffee and finds it tastes of burnt onion and margarine. He glances at his watch. Then he pays, smiles at Ricky as he thanks her for the change, which he hides for her under the saucer. This time he is careful not to stare at her as she walks away, though he does bestow an appreciative parting glance at her back and her hips. He can see through her skirt that the left side of her underpants is slightly higher than the right side. It is hard for him to tear his eyes away. Eventually he gets up to leave, then changes his mind and goes down the two steps to the windowless toilet: the dead light bulb, the peeling plaster and the smell of stale urine in the dark remind him that he isn't prepared for the meeting and has no idea how he will answer the audience's questions.

As he comes up from the toilet he sees that Mr. Leon and Shlomo Hougi have moved their chairs closer together and are now sitting shoulder to shoulder, bent over a notepad. The heavyset man runs his thick thumb slowly along the rows of numbers, while he talks in an emphatic whisper, shaking his head repeatedly, as though ruling something out once and for all, no question of it, while his acquiescent partner nods over and over again.

The Author steps out into the street and lights another cigarette. It's twenty past nine. The evening is hot and sticky, the congealed air lies heavy on streets and yards, saturated with soot and burnt gasoline. How terrible it must be, he thinks, on such a suffocating evening, to be lying in a critical condition in Ichilov Hospital, pierced with needles and connected up to tubes, between sweaty sheets, to the asthmatic sound of a bank of breathing machines. He pictures Ovadya Hazzam, before he got ill, an active man, always on the move, running all over the place, heavily built but agile, almost with a dancer's movements, driving around town in his blue Buick, always surrounded by helpers, friends, advice-givers, young girls, investors, wheeler-dealers and men on the make, throngs of people with ideas and initiatives, with favors to ask, and all kinds of fixers and meddlers. All day long he slapped people on the back, hugged men and women alike to his broad chest, punched them playfully in the ribs, gave his word of honor, expressed amazement, burst into roars of laughter, remonstrated, rebuked and cracked jokes, said I am completely stunned, shouted Forget it, what the hell, quoted biblical verses, and sometimes succumbed to a mounting wave of sentiment, and then he would start, with no prior warning, smothering men and women indiscriminately with kisses and eager caresses, almost going down on bended knees, suddenly bursting into tears, grinning shyly and kissing, caressing, hugging and weeping all over again, bowing deeply and promising never to forget, and then off he hurried, breathless, smiling, waving goodbye to you with an open hand that always had the keys to the Buick suspended from one finger.

Beneath the window of the terminal ward where Ovadya Hazzam is lying, the evening is punctuated by ambulance sirens, screeching brakes, a brutish babble of full-volume advertising slogans from the blaring radio in the taxi station at the entrance to the hospital. With every breath his lungs are invaded by a foul cocktail of smells: urine, sedatives, leftover food, sweat, sprays, chlorine, medicines, soiled dressings, excrement, beetroot salad, and disinfectant. In vain have all the windows been opened wide in the old cultural center now renamed for "Shunia Shor and the Seven Victims of the Quarry Attack": the air conditioning is out of order and the air is close and suffocating. The audience is drenched with sweat. Some bump into friends and stand chatting in the aisles. Others sit on hard seats, the younger ones on benches at the back because the older regulars have filled the front rows, their clothes sticking to their bodies, exuding their own smell and that of their neighbors into the murky air.

Meanwhile they exchange opinions, about the latest news, the terrible event in Acre, the leaks from the cabinet meeting, the revelations of corruption, the general situation, the air conditioning not working, and the heat. Three weary fans revolve ineffectually and almost unnoticed overhead: it is very hot here. Tiny insects squeeze between your collar and the back of your neck, like tropical Africa. Smells of sweat and deodorant hang in the air.

Outside, three or four streets away, the siren of an ambulance or fire engine rises and falls, an ominous wail that gradually fades, not so much because of the distance as from failing strength. The night is pierced by the staccato alarm of a parked car struck by sudden panic in the darkness. Will the Author say something new this evening? Will he manage to explain to us how we got into this state of affairs, or what we have to do to change it? Can he see something that we haven't seen yet?

Some have brought along the book that is the subject of this evening's event, and are using it — or a newspaper — to fan themselves. There's a delay and still no sign of the Author. The program includes words of welcome, a lecture by a literary critic, a reading of short extracts from the new work, the writer's talk, questions and answers, summing up, and closing remarks. Admission is free, and people are curious.

And here he is, at last, the writer.

The venue's cultural administrator has been waiting for him outside, at the foot of the stairs, for the past twenty minutes. He is a positive, affable man of about seventy-two, ruddy and round, with a face that reminds you of an apple that has been left too long in the fruit bowl until it turns wrinkly. Unhealthy-looking blue veins crisscross his cheeks. His spirit, though, is as lively as ever, like a fireman's hose aiming jets of enthusiasm and social commitment in every direction. But an acrid wave of body odor can be sensed from a handshake away. He wastes no time in starting to forge with the Author, who is thirty years his junior, bonds of affection erupting to mingle with big-hearted admiration, like the intimacy between two veteran guerrilla fighters: You and I, after all, struggle tirelessly, each in our own battle zone, for the promotion of values, of culture and of ideas, and to strengthen the ramparts of civilization. That is why we can permit ourselves, in private here, behind the scenes, a couple of minutes of light-hearted banter before we put on appropriately serious faces when we walk into the hall and take our places on the dais.

Well, well, well, welcome, my young friend, welcome, we've been waiting for you here like a bridegroom, hee-hee, you are, how can I put it, a little on the late side. What? You were held up in a café? Well, it's not the end of the world, everyone's always late here. Maybe you've heard the joke about the circumciser who was late for a circumcision? No. I'll tell you. Later. It's rather a long story, which by the way you can also find in Druyanov, you must be familiar with Druyanov? No? How so? And you a Jewish writer! Druyanov, Rabbi Alter Druyanov, the author of *The Book of Jokes and Witticisms*! But it's a veritable gold mine for any Jewish writer. Well, never mind. They're all out there waiting impatiently for us. We'll talk about Druyanov later. Definitely. But don't forget to remind me, I have a little thought of my own about the essential difference between a joke and a witticism. All right then, later. After all, you were a little late, my friend, never mind, it's not the end of the world, only we'd begun to fear that the muses had driven us out of your mind. But we didn't give up hope! No indeed, my dear friend! We are made of sterner stuff!

The Author, in his turn, apologizes for his lateness and murmurs a little witticism of his own: You could always have started without me. Hee-hee-hee. Without you! That's funny! The old culture-monger bursts out laughing, and his body odor is like the smell of fruit that is past its sell-by date. But, with all due respect, you could have started without us, too, in some other place. And by the way (both are out of breath as they climb the stairs), what do you think those American foxes will get out of their Arab friends? Will they manage to buy us a little peace and quiet at last? At least for a year or two?

He answers his own question: They won't get anything

out of it. They'll only bring us more troubles. As if the old ones weren't bad enough! Some juice? Lemonade? Maybe something fizzy? Be quick, though. Here, I'll choose for you — now, let's hope you'll give us a fizzy evening.

Drink up, in your own time, and then we'll go out there and take on our audience. They could do with shaking up, in my humble opinion. You can be as provocative as you like, my dear. Don't spare them! Right, if you've finished your drink, let's be getting out there. They must be cursing us by now.

And so the two of them, the Author and the old culture-merchant, step out of the wings in Indian file and walk toward the front of the stage, looking as solemn and serious as a pair of bailiffs. A rapid flurry of whispers runs round the hall, perhaps because the Author is wearing a summer shirt, khaki shorts, and sandals, and looks less like an artist than a kibbutznik who's been sent into town to organize a peace rally, or like a reserve army officer in mufti. They say that in his private life he's actually quite a simple guy, on a personal level, I mean, someone like you and me, and look what complicated books he comes up with. He probably had a difficult childhood. It would be interesting to know what he's like to live with. Not that easy, to judge by his books. They say he's divorced? Isn't he? Not just once but twice? You can tell from his books: there's no smoke without fire. Anyway, he looks completely different in his pictures. He's aged quite a bit. How old do you think he is? He must be forty-five or so, don't you think? Forty-five at the outside. You want to know the truth, I would have sworn, literally sworn, that he was taller than he is.

They put the Author in the middle, between the professional reader, who will read passages aloud from the Author's work, and the literary critic. They shake hands. They nod. Rochele Reznik withdraws her fingers from his clasp quickly, as though she's been burnt. The Author makes a mental note that the handshake made her slim neck blush more than her cheeks.

The cultural organizer gets to his feet heavily, tries out the microphone, and clears his throat. He starts by welcoming the very mixed and multi-generational audience gathered here this evening, he apologizes for the air conditioning not working, quipping that every cloud has a silver lining — the breakdown means that for once we don't have to put up with its infernal humming and so this time we will not miss one word.

Then he lists the program for this evening, promising the event will conclude with questions and answers, in the form of a no-holds-barred discussion with our guest whom, he declares gleefully, it is truly superfluous to introduce, despite which, to justify his presence, he spends the next ten minutes relating the Author's life story and listing all his books (erroneously attributing to his paternity a famous novel by another writer), and concludes his introductory remarks by repeating to the audience in his high-spirited way the Author's witticism on the staircase just now: our bridegroom of this evening was surprised to learn we had waited for him and not begun the program without him, hee-hee! Apropos of which it is not inappropriate to quote the well-known lines of the veteran poet Tsefania Beit-Halachmi, from his book *Rhyming Life and Death*, which goes something like this:

> *You'll always find them side by side:*
> *never a groom without a bride.*

Yes. And now, with your permission, we shall proceed to this evening's program. Good evening, everyone, and welcome to the monthly meeting of the Good Book Club at the refurbished Shunia Shor and the Seven Victims of the Quarry Attack Cultural Center. I am very pleased to be able to say that the Good Book Club has been meeting here on a regular basis every month for the past eleven and a half years.

The Author, listening to this, decides not to smile. He appears thoughtful, faintly sad. The audience's eyes are on him, but he, apparently paying no attention, deliberately fixes his gaze on the picture of the Labor leader Berl Katznelson on the wall to the right of the dais. Katznelson looks crafty but kindly, as though he has just pulled off a coup by devious means known only to himself. For now he is a king. A lord, even. And so, belatedly, the Author smiles that faint smile the audience has been waiting for since the cultural commissar's opening speech.

At that moment the Author has a feeling that somebody, somewhere in the furthest recesses of the hall, has
sniggered offensively. He scans the hall: nothing. There's
no one who looks as though he has just laughed. His ears
must have deceived him. So he rests his elbows on the table and his chin on his fists, and affects a modest, faraway
look while the literary critic, his freckled bald pate sparkling under the ceiling lights, stands and stridently draws
comparisons and parallels between the Author's latest book
and works by various contemporaries and writers of previous generations, tracing influences, identifying sources
of inspiration, revealing hidden textures, indicating various levels and planes, pointing up unexpected connec-
tions, plunging to the lowest depths of the story, digging
and burrowing in the ocean floor, then rising breathlessly
to the surface to display to the world the treasures he has
managed to bring up with him, then diving once more and
rising to the surface again to disclose concealed messages,
to reveal the ploys and devices the Author has used, such
as the strategy of the double negative, the snares and delu-
sions he has concealed in the lower layers of his plot, and
then on to the problem of credibility and reliability, which
raises the fundamental question of narrative authority,
and, in turn, the dimension of social irony and the elu-
sive boundary between this and self-irony, which brings us
to questions about the limits of legitimacy, the classifica-
tion of conventions, the intertextual context, from where
it is but a short step to the formalist aspects, the pseudo-

archaic aspects, and the contemporary political aspects. Are these various latent aspects legitimate? Are they even coherent? Are they synchronic or diachronic? Disharmonic or polyphonic? Eventually the critic weighs anchor and sails away boldly onto the open seas of wide-ranging meanings, but not before impressing his listeners with a nimble detour around the fundamental question, what is the actual meaning of the term "meaning" in relation to artistic creation in general and literary creation in particular, and of course in relation to the work we are considering this evening?

In vain.

By this time the Author is totally immersed in his usual tricks. Resting the palms of his hands on his temples (a gesture learned from his father, a minor diplomat), he stops listening and starts looking around the hall, to steal an embittered expression here, a lascivious one there, or a miserable one, to catch a pair of legs just as they uncross and are about to cross again, to seize a mop of unruly white hair, or a passionately expectant face, to spot a rivulet of perspiration running down deep into the crack between a pair of breasts. Over there, in the distance, next to the emergency exit, he can make out a pale, narrow, intelligent-looking face, like that of a student who has dropped out of a yeshiva and become, let us say, an enemy of the established social order. And here, in the third row, a suntanned girl with nice breasts, in a sleeveless green top, is absent-mindedly stroking her shoulder with her long fingers.

It is as though he were picking their pockets while the audience is immersed in the byways of his writing with the literary expert as their guide.

In the front, over there, a broad-faced, heavily built woman is sitting with her vein-lined legs wide apart, she has long ago abandoned any attempt at dieting, beauty is a delusion after all, she has given up caring about her appearance and determined to ascend to higher spheres. She does not take her eyes off the speaker, the literary expert, for a moment, her lips are parted with the sweetness of the cultural experience she is undergoing.

Almost in a straight line behind her a boy of about sixteen is moving restlessly on his chair; he looks unhappy, perhaps he is a budding poet, his face is pimply and his untidy hair looks like dusty steel wool. The torments of his age and the burden of his nightly practices have etched a tearful look on his face, and through his pebble lenses he loves this Author *de profundis*, secretly and passionately: my suffering is your suffering, your soul is my soul, you are the only one who can understand, for I am the soul that pines in solitude among the pages of your books.

On the other side of the hall from the boy sits a stocky figure with the distinct look of a trade-union hack, who ten or fifteen years ago was probably still an idealistic teacher in an old school in a working-class suburb now gentrified, perhaps even the retired deputy head of the regional educational department. His jawline looks squashed, his salt-and-pepper eyebrows are wild and bushy, and a cockroach-shaped birthmark nestles on his upper lip, just beneath his right nostril. The Author imagines that before the end of the session we shall have an opportunity to hear from this stout fellow a summary of his views: it is all but certain that he has come here this evening not to broaden his horizons or to enjoy himself but specifically so that he can rise to his feet after the speakers have had their say, thump on the table, and express once and for all his negative opinion of what is called "contemporary Hebrew literature," which contains nothing at all of what is needed at the present time, in the early 1980s, but unfortunately is crammed full of everything that we have no need of whatsoever.

The Author, for his part, decides to name the old teacher Dr. Pessach Yikhat. The waitress at the café he has called Ricky. The gangster's henchman will continue to be Mr. Leon while the name Shlomo Hougi still suits his stooping sidekick. The budding poet will be Yuval Dahan, but when he timidly sends his first poems to a literary editor he will sign himself Yuval Dotan. The culture-thirsty woman will be called Miriam Nehorait (the kids in her neighborhood call her Mira the Horror). The story will be set in an old building with peeling walls, on Reines Street in Tel Aviv. Slowly a frail bond will be established between Miriam Nehorait and the bespectacled boy. One morning he will be sent to her apartment on an errand by his mother. He will be treated to a glass of juice and two homemade bis-

cuits but will politely decline a third one and will also re-
fuse an apple. As he leaves he will mumble confusedly that
no, he doesn't play an instrument and that yes, he does
sometimes write a bit. Nothing much. Just odd efforts.

He turns up again a couple of days later, as she has invited him to show her his poems, which she finds not in
the least immature, on the contrary, they have an emotional depth, a richness of language, an aesthetic refine-
ment, and an immense love of humanity and of nature.
And this time the boy does accept an apple, which she
peels for him, as well as three biscuits and some juice.

A week later Yuval knocks on her door again. The following days too. Miriam Nehorait makes her sweet, sticky
fruit compote for him, and he shyly hands her a gift he has
bought, a fossilized snail imprisoned in a lump of pale blue
glass. On the following evenings she occasionally touches
his arm or his shoulder lightly while they talk. From surprise or else maternal tenderness she overlooks his hand
that once — and once only — climbs awkwardly, almost by
accident, up her dress to rest for the space of three or four
breaths, as though fainting, on her breast. It is at that very
moment that a neighbor, Lisaveta Kunitsin, happens to
look through her kitchen window, and so malicious gossip
snuffs out something that hardly happened, and it all ends
in disgrace. Miriam Nehorait goes on stewing her fruit
compote for him, as sweet as jam and as sticky as glue, she
lets it cool and keeps it in the refrigerator for him, but the
young Yuval Dotan never returns to her apartment, except
in his poems and his dreams, and in his murky nocturnal

fantasies, on account of which he makes up his mind that there is no reason to go on living, but he postpones the act until after this literary evening because he pins some vague hope on a meeting with the Author who will understand his affliction and will surely want to stretch out a friendly hand, and, who knows, may even invite him to his home, will be impressed by his poems, and after a while, when acquaintance has ripened into friendship and friendship has become a spiritual bond — at this point the fantasy becomes almost more miraculous and pleasurable than the boy can bear — the Author may open the doors of the world of literature to him. A wonderful, glittering world, a world that will eventually offer a dizzying recompense for the poet's suffering, rapt applause and the admiration of daintily swooning girls and the love of mature women burning to lavish on you everything you have touched in your dreams and things that even in your dreams you have not seen.

It might make sense to tell the story in the first person, from the point of view of one of the neighbors, Yerucham Shdemati, for example, the rotund cultural administrator who introduced you this evening and quoted the couplet from *Rhyming Life and Death* by Tsefania Beit-Halachmi.

> *You'll always find them side by side:*
> *never a groom without a bride.*

It's an airless summer evening, and Yerucham is relaxing in the dark, tired and sweaty, his ruddy face crisscrossed unhealthily by blue veins, sitting on a shabby easy chair on the balcony of his two-room apartment in a workers' housing development, with his swollen feet soaking in a bowl of cold water, casting his mind over the few memories he has left of his mother, who died in Kharkov sixty-six years ago, when he was only six (her name, like that of the gossipy neighbor, was Lisaveta). Right underneath his balcony a whispered conversation is going on. He ought to get up and go indoors at once, he has no right, no business, to eavesdrop on what they are saying to each other, but it is too late, because if he gets up now he will disturb the couple and embarrass himself. With no decent way out, Yerucham Shdemati goes on sitting uncomfortably on his balcony, but decides for the sake of decency to cover his ears with his thick hands. However, before doing so, he leans over the balcony and recognizes the silhouette of Yuval Dahan, his neighbors' shy teenage son, and the whispered lilt of Miriam Nehorait, which he cannot mistake because once, many years ago, on the night the Soviets sent the first sputnik into space, etc.

It might be possible to invest in the figure of the veteran cultural administrator one or two traits taken from the literary critic (who right now is expounding the paradox of changing points of view in the work): for example, he could contribute the semicircle of white hair that, Ben-Gurion fashion, adorns the latter's freckled head; his buzzing, rebarbative presence, like a swarm of angry bees;

perhaps even his triumphal delivery, like someone whose argument has just been conclusively rebutted but who, politely reining in his anger, does not give an inch but stuns his assailants with a doubly decisive riposte sealed with a courteous sting in its tail. The Author is inclined to give the lecturer twenty years as a widower and an only daughter, named Aya, who after perversely finding religion has married a settler from Elon Moreh in the West Bank. The name that suits him best is Yakir Bar-Orian (Zhitomirski). Such are the Author's peccadilloes while Bar-Orian reaches his peroration, in which he presents the work before us as a trap, as a hermetically sealed chamber of mirrors with no door or window. Just at this point a snigger is heard again in some corner of the hall, a strangled laugh full of mockery and despair, disturbing the Author and causing him to lose the thread of his subversive thoughts. Suddenly he is dying for a cigarette.

How about the poet Tsefania Beit-Halachmi, from whose book *Rhyming Life and Death* the cultural administrator in his opening remarks cited the couplet "You'll always find them side by side: / never a groom without a bride"? Is he still alive? It is years now since his verse stopped appearing in literary supplements and magazines. His very name is forgotten, except perhaps by a few residents of old people's homes. Yet once, when the Author was young, his poems were quoted at every ceremony, every celebration or public meeting.

Every human is God's creature
And God's spark is in him seen;
Each of us a microcosm,
Every heart contains its dream.

(This poem was played and sung to a melancholy Russian-style tune; a whole generation, the Author among them, sang it, in voices quivering with sadness and longing, around campfires and on kibbutz lawns. But now both the words and the tune have been forgotten. Just like the naive poet himself.)

When the jesting spirit descended upon him, Beit-Halachmi was capable of rhyming like this: "Only a horse / never questions his course," or "As babbling brooks flow to a pool / so are the words of a prattling fool."

When the Author was fifteen or so, a girl in his class at school (who was attractive rather than pretty) gave him a book called *Narcissus and Goldmund* by Hermann Hesse, and she wrote on the flyleaf these lines by Tsefania Beit-Halachmi:

The wind blows where it listeth,
And as it blows it sings:
Perchance this time the soaring wind
Will lift you on its wings.

Once Bar-Orian has concluded his discourse it is Rochele Reznik's turn to read out four short extracts from the Author's new book. She is pretty and shy, pretty yet not attractive, a slim, demure woman of thirty-five or so, with a single, dark old-fashioned plait falling over her shoulder and hiding her left breast.

She is wearing a cream cotton dress, sleeveless but buttoned up to the neck, printed with a pattern of blue or purple cyclamen. With her dress, her plait, and her demure bearing she looks to the Author like a pioneer girl left over from a previous generation. Or does she come from a religious background?

Rochele Reznik is standing facing the audience, her back slightly bent over the page, her forehead leaning toward the microphone, her slim forearms supporting your book as though it were a tray laden with glasses, and she reads as though there were nothing in your book except love and tenderness. Even the vitriolic dialogue that you wrote as though you were scattering shards of glass she reads with gentleness and feeling.

Why have you come here this evening, the Author asks himself, what can you get out of it? You ought to be at home right now, sitting at your desk, or lying on your back on the rug, making out shapes on the ceiling. What obscure demon drives you to come out again and again to these gatherings? Instead of being here, you could be sitting quietly at home, listening to Cantata BWV 106, the "Actus tragicus." You could have been an engineer designing railways for difficult mountain terrains, as you dreamed of doing when you were little. (When his father was serving as secretary at the embassy in Bogotá, the Author, then aged twelve, went on a trip in a mountainous region where the ramshackle train wound its way among dizzying drops, a journey that still haunts his dreams.)

And in fact why do you write? And for whom? What is your message, if any? What role do your books play and what good do they do anybody? What answers have you got to the important questions, or at least to some of them?

Compassion and grace, that is what Rochele Reznik finds in the pages you have written, and she is a pleasant and almost pretty girl, only not really attractive.

To one side, in one of the back rows, sits a boy — no, it's a man: gaunt, slightly shriveled, he looks like a monkey that has lost most of its fur and just has some tufts left on its sunken cheeks, a shabby man in his sixties, with a thinning crest of hair like an anemic cockscomb. He could be, let's say, a low-ranking activist who has been thrown out of the section office because he was caught passing confidential papers to an agent from another party, since then he has eked out a living by giving private math lessons.

Arnold Bartok would be a good name for him. A month ago he was sacked from his part-time job sorting parcels in a private courier company. His shirt collar is discolored by sweat and grime, his trousers hang loose from his hips, he hardly ever bothers to wash his shirts or his underwear, and his sandals are worn out. Arnold Bartok spends his evenings composing memos addressed to ministers, journalists and members of the Knesset, writes letters to the editors of various newspapers, pens urgent messages to the state comptroller or the president, and he suffers terribly from piles. Specially in the early hours.

He lives with his mother, Ophelia, whose legs are paralyzed. The two of them sleep under the same sheet on a worn-out mattress in their room, which is no more than a windowless cubicle that was once his father's little laundry. Since his father died the iron shutters of the laundry have been permanently closed and secured with a padlock, and the only entrance is at the rear, from the yard, through a warped plywood door. The toilets are in a corrugated-iron lean-to at the other end of the yard, but they are out of reach for the disabled widow, who is dependent on an enamel chamber pot that Arnold Bartok has to put under her every hour or two and then go out and empty in the cracked toilet bowl in the lean-to, and wash under the tap between the trash cans. Black spots have appeared where the enamel of the chamber pot is worn or chipped, so that even after being washed and scrubbed and disinfected with bleach the pot always looks dirty.

For years now his mother has refused to address him by his proper name, Arnold, but maliciously insists on calling him Araleh or Arke, and when he remonstrates, Stop it, Mama, that's enough, you know very well that my name is Arnold, his paralyzed mother, coquettish as a spoilt little girl, cries exultantly from behind her glasses: What, again? What happened now? What's the matter with you, Araleh? Why you so angry with me? You want maybe to beat me a little? Like what your sainted father, God rest his soul, used to do? Is that what you want, Araleh? You want to beat me, huh?

Is Arnold Bartok the wretch who has just chuckled or sniggered again, for the third or fourth time? Is it deliberate mockery, the Author asks himself, or jealousy? Or disgust? Or anger? Or perhaps this is the abstract, depersonalized sound of suffering itself?

The Author tries to imagine Arnold Bartok, in nothing but his sweaty underwear, at a quarter to three at night in the damp, moldy laundry, pulling the smelly chamber pot out from underneath his mother's body, then panting with the effort as he turns her on her front to wipe her clean and fit her with a dry pad.

And so, when he is finally invited to speak, the Author appears at his best, and replies to the audience's questions patiently, modestly, and seriously. Occasionally he uses simple analogies or examples from everyday life. He takes his time as he expounds the difference between explaining and telling a story. He cites in passing Cervantes, Gogol, Balzac, and even Chekhov and Kafka. He tells a few anecdotes that reduce the audience to laughter. He launches a few sly digs at the literary critic, while he praises his presentation and thanks him for the profundity of his observations. As he speaks, he is amazed at everything: that he agreed to take part in this event, that he has not prepared for it properly, amazed at the words that are coming out of his mouth, even though as he pronounces them it is totally clear to him that he does not agree with what he is saying, and worse than that, the truth is he does not have the faintest shadow of an answer to the real, central questions, and he has no intrinsic interest in the things that his mouth is pouring forth, independently of him.

Nor does he have any idea as yet why Arnold Bartok bothered to come. Was it really just so as to sit at the back of the hall, stretch out his lizard's neck toward you and mock you with stifled sniggers? Isn't he quite right though to scoff? the Author says to himself, as, with his warm, gushing words, he continues to captivate his audience, especially the women.

He pauses for a moment and runs his fingers through his hair, remembering the waitress, Ricky, and her first love, Charlie, the reserve goalkeeper of Bnei-Yehuda football team who used to part her lips slowly with the tip of his nose, melting her until she almost fainted, and whispered Gogog to her, and even bought her, in Eilat, a dress with sparkling silvery sequins, an evening dress like a singer's from a hotel on the Riviera, before dumping her and taking up again with a girl called Lucy who was runner-up in the Queen of the Waves contest: men can't help themselves, that's just the way they are made, but women, in Ricky's view, are actually not much better, definitely not, women often have this thing where they act like lying cats that need to be petted, so the truth is that in any relationship there's not much to choose between the man and the woman, they're both pretty worthless. It's like this: if there's no electricity there, how on earth can they start to make a relationship? But if there is electricity then they end up getting burnt. And that's the reason why, Ricky thinks, one way or another love affairs always end in despair. But maybe with a bit of luck I'll manage to meet up with that Lucy? We'll have plenty to talk about, replay some juicy episodes, have a laugh together over things that were so painful all those years ago. I ought to try to find out where she's ended up, that Lucy, after being runner-up in the Queen of the Waves competition. Assuming she's still alive. And assuming she's living on her own, too. Like me. And assuming she doesn't mind meeting up with me.

With an expression that combines loneliness, cultural sensitivity, and sadness, the Author piles lie upon lie. To the questions from the audience, Why do you write, etc.? he gives answers he's already used more than once before, some of them clever, some witty or evasive. Tricks he learned from his father, the minor diplomat. By way of conclusion, he amusingly throws the ball back to the cultural administrator, Yerucham Shdemati, and repays him in his own coin with some lines from *Rhyming Life and Death:*

> *Many a wise man lacks for sense,*
> *Many a fool has a heart of gold,*
> *Happiness often ends in tears,*
> *But what's inside can never be told.*

Then he is surrounded by his readers. Nonchalantly he signs copies of his latest book, accepts praise with an air of pensive modesty, occasionally smiling a smile that looks like a stifled yawn, while attempting to assuage the ire of Dr. Pessach Yikhat, the broad-jawed, cantankerous educator with bushy gray eyebrows and hair sprouting out of his ears and nostrils, assuring him that contemporary literature does not all negate the State: condemning the injustices of the occupation, satirizing corruption and widespread brutishness, exposing decadence and stupidity, these things do not amount to negating the State, often, in fact, they come from a broken heart. Even if the enemies of Israel sometimes exploit things that are written here for their own ends, that definitely doesn't indicate, and after all the biblical prophets too, etc., and also earlier modern writers like Bialik or Brenner, Uri Zvi Greenberg or S. Yizhar, etc., etc.

The Author generously allows the boy with the pebble lenses, Yuval Dahan or Dotan, to send him some of his poems. Send them, yes do, but please be patient and don't expect a reply in a day or two, you must understand that loads of people send me their stuff and ask my opinion of it, but sadly my time, etc., etc.

Then with a wink he shakes hands firmly with Yakir Bar-Orian Zhitomirski, the expert on literature, he thanks Yerucham Shdemati, the cultural administrator, who thanks him in turn for agreeing to come and speak, No thanks, there's really no need to call a taxi, I'm staying nearby tonight, I'd rather walk back, it'll refresh me, maybe a sea breeze has started to blow and it may get cooler soon?

Outside on the stairs the Author lights a cigarette and devotes his attention to Rochele Reznik. He thanks her warmly, and praises the sensitivity of her reading and her pleasant voice. She, for her part, gives an embarrassed smile, as if instead of being complimented she has been unfairly reprimanded, and in a choked voice she thanks him for his kind words: it is not she who deserves the praise, but the book she has read from.

When the Author stands aside to let her pass she murmurs repeatedly, It's nothing, thank you, really, it's nothing. Then, as though she has offended him, she says sadly, No thank you, I don't smoke, I'm sorry, thank you anyway, no really. And she holds the book she has read from in front of her like a breastplate, wrapped in brown paper kept in place by two rubber bands.

You know, the Author says, the truth is that I would have been very happy if instead of all the talking this evening they had just let you read, I mean if the whole evening had just been a reading, instead of all the nitpicking, the exposition and analysis, and even my own wisecracks at the end. You really read my words from the inside, as though you were inside the book and not just holding it open in front of you. When you read, the book itself begins to speak.

Don't mention it, Rochele Reznik mumbles, it's nothing, thank you, really, it's nothing. Then it suddenly dawns on her that that was not the right way to reply, and she apologizes in a voice close to tears.

At this moment the light on the staircase goes out, and the Author tries to hold her arm to steady her, while feeling with his other hand for the light button, but in the darkness his fingers alight for a moment on the warmth of her breast, before encountering the banister. Meanwhile someone on another floor has turned the light on. The Author apologizes and Rochele Reznik, somewhat surprised, replies in a tremulous voice, Don't mention it, it's nothing, thank you, really, thank you very much. I'm sorry if I'm a bit emotional. The Author continues: Besides which, your voice really sounds to me so much like the inner voice of the character as I heard it while I was writing.

Rochele Reznik receives this in silence, her lips trembling. Eventually she says, with downcast eyes, that she has to admit she was very nervous before this evening, she was frankly terrified, after all, reading extracts from an author's work in his presence is a bit like playing Schubert when Schubert is sitting in the hall.

The Author offers to walk Rochele Reznik home: he feels like taking a stroll anyway, and breathing the night air, and they could chat on the way or maybe sit down somewhere and have a hot or cold drink. Or even something stronger?

Now she is thrown completely off balance, she blushes from her ears to her neck, as if her dress has suddenly come unzipped, she apologizes, confused, unfortunately there's really nowhere to walk her, because she happens to live right here, opposite the community center, just up there, under the roof, that window on the left, the one with no light on, she's really terribly sorry, no, she's not sorry, but . . . well. It just so happens this is where I live. Upstairs.

If there's no light on, the Author smiles, that must be a sign that there's nobody waiting for you so you can still come for a walk?

No, Joselito is waiting for me, I think he must be looking at the clock every few minutes by now, if I'm only a little bit late he always gets angry with me and gives me a guilt trip, where have you been, what did you do, how could you, you should be ashamed of yourself.

Joselito?

A cat. A devil in cat's clothing.

But the Author does not give up. Why don't we go for a walk anyway before you climb up to that roof of yours? Then I'll have a word with this Joselito. I'll give you a note for him. Or should I grease his little paw with a bribe for you? Just let me take you to a special place that's less than five minutes from here? It's very near, at the end of the street and then to the left, come with me and let me show you something and tell you a little story (holding her elbow lightly now, almost absentmindedly). Here, look, right here, on the spot where they've put up this boutique, many years ago stood the Pogrebinsky Brothers' pharmacy, where once, when I was six years old, my Uncle Osya, my mother's brother, left me behind, he simply forgot me, and it was more than an hour later that he came back, shouting at Madame Pogrebinskaya, the pharmacist, What sort of irresponsible behavior is that, roaring at me, *Ti paskudniak*, little devil, don't you dare disappear like that again, waving his fist at me and threatening to hit me. But before Uncle Osya came back, when I was alone with the pharmacist and the intoxicating smells, she had taken me into a dark little back room and explained to me in a whisper about all sorts of drugs and poisons and how they all work. Ever since then I have had a weakness for poisons and I'm fascinated by cellars, storerooms and all sorts of secret cubbyholes. (While he is talking, the Author releases her elbow but drapes his arm over her shoulder. She trembles, doesn't know what she should do or say, and decides to do nothing.)

Tell me, am I boring you?

No, of course you're not boring me, what a thought! Rochele Reznik exclaims in alarm. For me this is an experience, it's as though you're giving me a preview of your next story, one you haven't written yet. Or even one that you've started and haven't finished. Of course, you don't have to tell me. I'm sorry I asked, you should never ask a writer questions like that. (He removes his arm, but first squeezes her shoulder and presses her to him.)

Very carefully, as though walking barefoot in the dark, Rochele Reznik continues, Take me, for instance, I don't believe in coincidences anymore. There have been moments lately when I've had a sudden feeling that everything that happens — literally everything, without exception . . . but I'm not sure I can explain. Don't you ever think that nothing, I mean nothing, happens by chance?

> *A budding shoot, a falling leaf,*
> *A baby born, an old man dead,*
> *Say not it's chance — a vain belief,*
> *But put it down to fate instead.*

The Author cites these forgotten lines by Tsefania Beit-Halachmi that have suddenly popped up in his memory. Rochele Reznik says: I actually met him several times, at various family celebrations. He had a pink, round face, like a blancmange, with very red lips, always smiling, like a cherry in the middle of the blancmange, and soft fingers that smelled of perfume and were always pinching children's cheeks in a limp, unpleasant way.

Who?

Beit-Halachmi. The poet. His real name wasn't Tsefania, it wasn't Beit-Halachmi either. It was something totally different, something like Avraham Schuldenfrei. Bumek. We just called him Uncle Bumek. Once my mother replaced the actress who always read for him, because she had sinusitis, so my mother read at an evening in honor of Uncle Bumek in Kiryat Chayim. And even that night, although I wasn't a little girl anymore, I was already in the army by then, he pinched my cheeks limply every five minutes, and once he pinched me somewhere else too. He was vaguely related to us — I'm not sure exactly how. He wasn't a real uncle, maybe he was an uncle of one of my parents' in-laws. Or their great-uncle, perhaps. At family gatherings when I was little they used to say to me, look over there, you see that man shaking hands and smiling left and right, the one who looks like an overgrown pudgy baby, that's our Uncle Bumek, who's also the famous poet Tsefania Beit-Halachmi.

And to a question from the Author she replies: I don't know. I'm not sure. I haven't heard anything about him for ages. It's possible he's still alive. But I may be wrong, no, he can't be, because if he were still alive he'd have to be about a hundred.

Giving her a sidelong glance, the Author notices that her front teeth are slightly protruding and rather widely spaced, like a squirrel whose attention is fixed on something but whose fur is already rippling with fear: any moment now she will run off to her rooftop room and her jealous cat.

Casually, lightly, he puts his arm round her waist, as though here too there are stairs she may trip and fall on, Come on, don't be frightened, Rochele. Shall we take a peep into the yard at the back? Maybe that little back room still exists. Maybe there's a window, let's take a look and see what's still there, if anything. Clumsily she pulls herself free of his embrace, and at once, as though regretting this, she says boldly, Yes, I'll come, show me.

But in the backyard lit faintly by yellowish light from kitchens there is only broken furniture, an abandoned baby carriage, some cardboard boxes, smells of cooking and rubbish, twisted blinds, the sound of flushing toilets, shrieks and laughter blaring from TVs, groaning air-conditioning units, and the scampering of a startled cat.

The Author mutters a few confused sentences about the fog of passing time and the maze of memory, while absent-mindedly stroking her hair, down to the base of her plait, then takes her by the shoulders and draws her gently toward him. But his new book, wrapped in brown paper secured by two rubber bands, separates him from her flat chest like a shield. Suddenly, in a high, girlish, quivering voice, like a baby bird's, so different from the warm voice she read in earlier, she says: I'm a little scared.

At once he lets go of her, he remembers that she is not that young and that she's not really attractive, what's got into him all of a sudden, he mumbles an apology, lights another cigarette and walks her back to her home opposite the cultural center. On the way he tries to make amends for what almost didn't happen by telling her amusing stories, one after another. Like the story of the woman who rang his doorbell one day. She was a short woman with broad shoulders, wearing heavy glasses and a green-and-white-striped pantsuit. She was clutching, almost violently, the arm of a child of about nine who kept trying to break free from her grasp. Excuse me for ringing your bell like this, sir, and disturbing you, the fact is we don't really know each other — that is, everyone knows you of course, but not us, come on, Sagiv, say hallo nicely to the famous writer. We really don't want to disturb you, it won't take a moment, I'm a professional dietician, and many years ago I managed to speak to the famous poet Mrs. Lea Goldberg at the grocer's, but Sagiv here has never seen a real live writer. It's very important for him to see a writer, because one day he's going to grow up to be a very famous poet or writer. Sagivi? Come on? Tell the famous writer something very original and beautiful. No? What's the matter with you? But you prepared so beautifully at home. We even rehearsed it together. So how come you're suddenly so shy with the writer gentleman? There's no need to be shy. Writers understand our souls perfectly. Isn't that right? But we're sorry, we really don't want to intrude, we're leaving, we'll just leave this envelope with you please and we'll wait patiently for you to write us a letter. Write to us please and tell us your honest opinion of Sagivi's work. What could he improve? Maybe the ideas? Or the spelling? The style, maybe? Or maybe it would be better for him to tackle more practical subjects? And please, where can we publish it? What's come over you, Sagivi? Why don't you speak up and say your piece? What an idiot child! Excuse me, sir, if you could please write us just a recommendation? Or an introduction? With the fine recommendation you'll write for us please, anyone will agree to publish us!

Then the Author tells Rochele Reznik about his eccentric Uncle Osya, the one who forgot him in the Pogrebinsky Brothers' pharmacy. How this Uncle Osya once delivered a resounding slap on the cheek to the communist member of the Knesset, Shmuel Mikunis, how the two of them eventually ended up becoming bosom friends and how they even cared for each other devotedly when both fell ill the same year, the same month, with the same disease, and were even put in the same ward in the Ichilov Hospital.

For a moment the Author thinks of the dying Ovadya Hazzam, the man who lived like a king (a lord, even), had a wild time, came into money, got divorced, cruised around town all day in a blue Buick with blondes from Russia, slapped everyone on the shoulder, laughing and joking, belched thunderously, hugged and kissed everyone he met, even strangers, men and women alike, and when he burst out laughing he made the windowpanes rattle, and now in Ichilov his catheter has slipped out and the night nurse is too far away to hear his faint groan, so he lies there in a puddle of his warm, sour, bloodstained urine, which will soon cool down and run onto his belly, his groin, his back, making his buttocks stick to the wet sheet.

When they reach the entrance to Rochele Reznik's building the Author takes his leave of her warmly, thanks her for coming for a little walk with him, repeats his kind words about her reading, and offers to accompany her upstairs to her rooftop. She blushes under the cover of darkness and mumbles that there's really no need, Joselito is waiting for her up there, she always comes home alone, that is —

The Author insists, declaring in his most authoritative voice that everyone knows it's precisely on the staircases of old buildings in Tel Aviv at night that all sorts of things recently, etc. To be on the safe side he should definitely accompany her to her own front door, hand her over to her Joselito, not to mention keys getting lost or breaking off in the lock.

Rochele Reznik, embarrassed, stammers that there's really no need, thank you anyway, but there is really and truly no need, she simply turns on the light here, at the bottom of the stairs, and in two minutes she'll be home, Joselito is waiting by the door and he'll certainly kill her for coming home so late, apart from which, she's sorry but it so happens that it's not very cozy this evening in her apartment, because she's sent the curtains to be cleaned and there are no shutters, so the neighbors can —

At this she is smitten with panic mixed with shame: the curtains are not at the cleaners', they are precisely where they should be, and anyway why mention curtains? Why did I say to him that it's not very cozy this evening in the apartment? I even said that the neighbors could see everything. What on earth will he make of that? Have I gone out of my mind? What will he think I'm thinking? After all, he didn't even invite himself in, he just offered to go up the stairs with me and at the very most stand with me while I open the door to make sure the key hasn't got lost or doesn't stick or break off in the lock. And I made up a lie so he wouldn't come in. Even though the thought never even crossed his mind. And then I said that there are no shutters, and that the neighbors . . . You could infer that I was hinting to him that if only I did have curtains or shutters . . .

But what if he really did mean to imply that he'd like me to ask him in, for a chat and a drink? In which case, the moment he sets foot inside he'll see that the curtains are actually there. That they haven't gone to the cleaners'. And then? He'll realize at once that I simply lied to him for no reason. Where on earth can I hide myself?

Besides, she has no idea whether or not she really wants this Author, who is famous but so polite, even fatherly, that she is not entirely at her ease with him, to come upstairs with her. Yes, he wants something, but what does he really want from her? Does she want to invite him into her room or is she afraid to? Now? And did she or didn't she leave a black bra hanging on the back of her chair when she came out? And which side of the chair? What if it's hanging so that you can see at once that it's padded?

The light on the stairs goes out again and again the Author presses the switch, and says: Maybe I should, after all? To be on the safe side? Just as far as your door?

But now that she has lied to him and told him that the

curtains are at the cleaners', it's too late. There's no question. No way back. She has blocked all her own escape routes. There's no way she can let him come into her room and see that the curtains are hanging at the window as usual. She would die of shame.

In a faint voice, like a little girl who has been told off, she finally says to the Author: All right then, thank you, come upstairs with me, but only as far as the door . . . if you insist . . . but the truth is, though, that Joselito, I mean, he's not used to —

Then, suddenly aware of what she has just said, she falls silent, panic-stricken and helpless.

The Author observes her look of a hunted animal, of a terrified baby rodent, a cornered squirrel ready to bite itself in desperation. So he smiles and politely withdraws his offer: No, no, really, it doesn't matter, look, if it makes you feel so uncomfortable —

Now the squirrel is silenced, unable to decide which is worse, accepting his original offer to accompany her to her door, or accepting gratefully his polite withdrawal of the offer. Or should she ask him in, even though he may not be interested in an invitation, but simply offered to accompany her out of politeness or a genuine concern for her welfare? Or could she still not ask him in? Even though now that seems like the only option, and he might be offended? In which case, how can she cover her shame over the curtains? And the bra on the back of the chair? Besides which, there are little hairs everywhere from Joselito, who is starting to shed his fur now that the summer is here. And suppose the Author needs to use the bathroom suddenly, and what if she left the razor she has been using to rid herself of excess body hair out on the shelf?

Lowering her eyes to the pavement or to her shoes, she clutches the book to her chest, not knowing what to say.

The Author, of course, is aware of her distress. Lightly touching her shoulder, he courteously suggests: Look, if you feel like it, why don't we take another short stroll? Just to the end of the street and back? Or as far as the square? Of course, if you prefer to go up right away, without the services of a bodyguard, then if you don't mind I'll just stand here in the entrance until I hear your door open and close, so I know that you've made it safely back to your Joselito without meeting any dragons on the way.

With a twisted smile, close to tears, she mutters: I'm sorry. I don't know what's come over me. I'm a bit confused this evening.

The Author, too, smiles as he says to her in the dark: But so charming, too.

Nine or ten years have passed since someone, a boy, not a particularly attractive one, said something similar to her. He was a fast talker, and she didn't believe him. But now, this man, suddenly —

The blood once more flushes her ears and neck, and she feels as though her knees are melting and she has no choice, she must either lean on him or collapse.

Her knuckles show white as she clutches his book, in its brown paper and rubber bands, to her belly. Like a chastity belt. At that instant she almost summons up the courage to invite him upstairs, why not, what do the bra and the cat hairs matter, he must have seen the insides of a thousand girls' rooms in his time, she'll make him some tea, or coffee, she even has some Argentinean yerba mate, if he's not feeling too tired? Or isn't in a hurry to go somewhere?

But her lips can't help trembling in the darkness. Eventually, almost in a mumble, she reveals to him that she has a collection of matchboxes from two hundred hotels all round the world, well, maybe only a hundred and eighty, but why should a man like him be interested in a collection of matchboxes?

The Author lights another cigarette, pushes the light button again, and thinks it over. For an instant he has a mental image of the exciting asymmetry he spotted earlier in the evening, through her skirt, between the two sides of Ricky's (the waitress's) underpants: the left side was a little higher than the right. Like a wink promising an Aladdin's cave of secret thrills.

For a moment he weighs up the pros and cons in his mind: is it worth his while to be invited upstairs now to Rochele Reznik's rooftop room? Actually, why not? After all, her shy presence gives him pleasure, and he finds her tremulous praise quite enjoyable, and her fear is as sweet as the shivering of a little chick in the palm of one's hand: so why not? She won't eat him alive up there. On the other hand, even though she is almost stunned and even submissive she isn't that attractive. Either way, it'll end up being embarrassing: she is in a panic and he doesn't really fancy her. First he'll have to allay her fears, calm her down, like a patient family doctor with a girl who refuses to have an injection. And all the way he'll have to be so careful, so paternal that even the small amount of desire that he's been trying his hardest to boost with images of Ricky the waitress's underpants will fade. Either way, he'll have to pretend. He'll have to put on a performance for her, one way or another. Or make up an excuse. And he'll have to stroke her cat and say what lovely fur it has. He's had enough of showmanship for one night. And one way or another she, Rochele Reznik, will end up being hurt by him. Or worse still, she'll start nursing all sorts of hopes for a sequel. Which is totally out of the question.

Besides, she has no curtains and no shutters, and God knows who her neighbors are, and he is quite a well-known personality.

And so the Author entertains doubts, and the first question, Why not, is replaced in his mind by other questions. Why? Why the hell? What for? Is it just the old cliché of that wretched rhyme, "You'll always find them side by side: / never a groom without a bride"?

He reflects that Chekhov has already mapped out the route by which one can approach a strange lady by paying court to her lapdog. But even Chekhov did not explain to us how, once you have established acquaintance and got into conversation, you proceed from there. How, for example, do you get close to a girl who clutches a jealous cat to her breast, a growling bundle of fur that will surely scratch anyone who attempts to usurp its place?

And so the Author takes his leave on a note of controlled warmth. He promises to phone her, yes, definitely, very soon. By the light of the street lamp he hurriedly strokes her plait, and tries to look her straight in the eyes, but her eyes are once more lowered in the direction of the tips of her shoes or the cracked pavement. Rochele Reznik, a hunted squirrel with an expression of panic on her small face, also looks as though she may bite, perhaps because of the way her front teeth protrude. She suddenly proffers a tiny, cold hand for a hasty handshake; the other hand still presses his new book, wrapped in brown paper secured with two rubber bands, to her chest. While she withdraws her hand from his with an almost imperceptible movement that suggests a day-old chick, she suddenly smiles sadly and says: Goodnight, and thank you for everything. Thank you very much, really. And there's something else I wanted to say, I don't know how to put it, I just wanted to tell you that I don't think I'll ever forget this evening. I'll never forget the pharmacy and the back room with the poisons, or your uncle who slapped the member of the Knesset and then they both became ill.

The Author roams the streets for an hour or an hour and a half. His feet lead him away from the well-lit avenue to side streets, and unfamiliar alleyways, where all the shutters are barred and only an occasional anemic street lamp sleepily casts a murky glow. As he walks he smokes two more cigarettes and does the sum in his head: seven or eight since the start of the evening.

Two couples, their arms round one another, cross his path on their way to bed from a night out, and one of the girls lets out a shriek of horror, as though someone has whispered some outrageous possibility to her. The Author tries to imagine this possibility in detail, turning it round and round, looking for some kind of juicy excitement in it, but the incubus of the airless dungeon where Arnold Bartok and his mother Ophelia are shut away on their bed that is damp with sweat kills his nascent desire even before it can arise: the elderly mother and her middle-aged son are both stewing in their sweat on a single shapeless mattress, a skinny, veiny body straining to lift a massive heap of flabby flesh, and to push the chamber pot underneath — like a pair of wrestlers in the dark, the son grunting and the mother groaning, while a mosquito hums in the darkness like a tiny drill, there, or here, or both here and there.

Uncle Osya, the anarchist, the piano tuner, lived all alone in a small back room in the basement of an old building on Brenner Street, he was generally out of work, sometimes he took an odd job as a mover or a house painter, and even when he was in his thirties — a pudgy albino — everyone always called him "Oska-nu-kak," meaning "Well, Oska, how's it going?," and they jokingly said of him that in the recesses of his subterranean hideout he concealed the beautiful niece of the ousted Soviet leader Leon Trotsky from the British authorities and from the party.

Even as a child the Author knew that this was only a joke, that there were no beauties hidden in his eccentric uncle's basement, but now, for an instant, he is suddenly sorry that he never had the courage to peep behind the moldy greenish oilcloth that hung from wall to wall, concealing the innermost sanctum of the basement.

And he regrets his cowardice: why didn't you invite yourself up to Rochele Reznik's room? Behind that shy pallor of hers there probably lurks a feverish thirst, a blend of childlike innocence, unfulfilled desire, and a kind of silent, passionate submissive devotion flowing from her admiration and gratitude. It was right there at your fingertips, it was throbbing softly in the palm of your hand, and you let it escape. Idiot.

As for the poet Tsefania Beit-Halachmi, Bumek Schuldenfrei, the Author does the sums and concludes that he must have passed away long since. Many years ago he had his own regular poet's corner on the back page of the weekend supplement of the newspaper *Davar*, surrounded with a flowery border adorned in each corner with a sketch of a smiling mask. Or maybe it was sneering. The poems in *Rhyming Life and Death*, as the Author recalls, were not satirical or mordant, but generally addressed the problems of the day with good-natured if somewhat condescending amusement: absorption of immigrants, transit camps, austerity measures, the conquest of the desert, the draining of the Huleh swamp, the housing shortage, border incidents and raids by infiltrators, the corruption and bureaucracy that overshadowed the public life of the young State. He represented the younger generation, the muscular, suntanned native-born sabras, as outwardly tough but dedicated, morally responsible and wonderfully sensitive on the inside.

All the enemies of the Jewish people down the ages — the Ukrainians, the Poles, the Germans, the Arabs, the British, the priests, the effendis, the Bolsheviks, the Nazis, the innumerable anti-Semites that are spawned everywhere — were portrayed in *Rhyming Life and Death* as heartless villains whose world is filled with nothing but malice, hatred and schadenfreude directed against us. The homegrown villains, such as the dissident Zionist organizations, the Communists, the detractors of the trade-union movement and the opponents of the organized Jewish community, appeared in Beit-Halachmi's book as petty, narrowminded people with twisted souls. He thoroughly abhorred those bohemians who aped the ways of Paris and Hollywood, and he had nothing but disgust for all those cynical, uprooted intellectuals who knew only how to pour scorn and sarcasm on everything, together with their scribbles about modern art, which amounted to no more than the emperor's new clothes.

As for the Yemenites, animals, tillers of the soil and gentle children, for these he reserved verses radiant with paternal affection. He placed them on a pedestal, going into raptures over the purity of their innocence and the simplicity of their souls. But occasionally Tsefania Beit-Halachmi's rhymed column was infused with a hint of something that was neither political nor ideological, a mysterious tinge of sorrow that had nothing whatever to do with his class consciousness or patriotic fervor, like those lines the Author had quoted at the reading:

> *Many a wise man lacks for sense,*
> *Many a fool has a heart of gold,*
> *Happiness often ends in tears,*
> *But what's inside can never be told.*

Sometimes he included a short epitaph for someone who was dead and forgotten except in the occasional thoughts of a child or grandchild, and even this memory was ephemeral because, with the death of the last person who remembered him, the subject of the poem would die a second and final death.

Once, the Author recalls, Beit-Halachmi published a piece under the heading "Clearing out the Leaven," about the tendency of all things gradually to fade, to become worn out, objects and loves, clothes and ideals, homes and feelings, everything becomes tattered and threadbare, and eventually turns to dust.

He made frequent use of the word "alone," which on occasion he replaced with the rarer word "forlorn."

Once upon a time, in the thirties and forties and even perhaps in the early fifties, the poet used to appear frequently on Friday evenings before a crowd of his fans in cultural centers, Health Fund sanatoria, trade-union gatherings or meetings of the Movement for Popular Education: he would read from his poems, accompanied by a lady pianist who was no longer in the first flush of youth or an emotional Russian singer with a deep contralto voice and a generous but not indecent décolleté. After his reading and the musical interludes, he would enjoy chatting with his audience, debating good-naturedly, pinching the cheeks of the children and sometimes of grown women, he would sign copies of his books and revel in the affection of his public, many of whom in those days could recite entire poems of his by heart.

And then what happened? Perhaps, for example, his wife died one morning in an accident with an electric iron. And the poet waited a year and a half before marrying his big-bosomed accompanist. Who abandoned him two weeks after the wedding and ran away to America with her sister's brother-in-law, a cosmetics manufacturer with a pleasing tenor voice.

Or perhaps he is still alive, the poet Tsefania Beit-Halachmi? Totally forgotten, he drags out the remainder of his days somewhere, let's say in a remote, private old folks' home in a workers' village at the edge of the Hefer

Valley. Or in some godforsaken nursing home on the outskirts of Yokneam. His toothless mouth gums a piece of white bread to a pulp. He spends hours on end sitting in a brown armchair with an upholstered footstool on the veranda of the home where he lives; his mind is still as clear as ever but it is many years since he saw any point in writing poems or publishing them in the paper, now he is happy with a glass of tea and the quiet of the garden, the changing shapes of the clouds, and he still enjoys, in fact he enjoys more and more, observing the colors of the trees in the garden and inhaling the smell of freshly mown grass:

> *It's green and peaceful here, a crow*
> *stands on a pillar, all alone,*
> *a pair of cypress trees together*
> *and another on its own.*

All day long he sits in his armchair on the veranda, reading with curiosity a novel by a young writer who grew up in a religious community but abandoned the commandments, or the memoirs of the founder of a charitable organization. His eyesight is still good and he does not need glasses to read. Suddenly he comes across his own name mentioned in passing in the book, together with a couple of his old rhymes, which suddenly afford the old poet a childish pleasure, and he smiles and moves his lips as he reads the lines of verse: he himself has almost forgotten them, and he supposed, without rancor, that everyone else has forgotten them too, but here they are in the book by this young woman, and he finds them not bad at all.

His innocent, round eyes are blue and clear under his white eyebrows, like twin mountain pools surmounted by snowy crags, his body that used to be rotund is now as skinny as a child's, smooth and hairless, wrapped in a white flannel dressing gown printed with the logo of the old folks' home and the motto "Young at heart!" A small bubble of saliva appears in the corner of the poet's mouth, on the left side. Every two or three hours the nurse, Nadia, brings him a glass of lemon tea and a sugar lump, and a slice of white bread with the crust removed. He sits peacefully for hours on end without moving, placidly breathing the country air and smelling the smells, with faint snorts, chewing his bread pulp, dozing, or wide awake, with the book by the young woman from the religious neighborhood lying open face down on his lap, thinking about her and wondering whether death can be entirely, unrecognizably different from life. Surely there must be some resemblance, at least a hint of a resemblance, between the time before and after death, because there is after all a hint of a resemblance between any two times or situations in the world. Maybe that is how the poet sits all day staring with his thoughtful blue eyes at the swaying of the treetops and the movement of the clouds.

But a simple calculation shows that it is hardly possible that this poet is still alive. His weekly column, "Rhyming Life and Death," ceased to appear many years ago. The weekend supplement of *Davar* is on its last legs. The trade-union movement, the Histadrut, is no longer what it was. Instead of workers' councils with cultural commissions with a sense of mission and a moral obligation to go out to the ordinary people and raise their cultural level, the country is full of clever manpower resource companies and slave dealers who import herds of maids and forced laborers from poor countries.

Probably this poet passed away long ago, died of a cerebral hemorrhage and was hastily buried one windy, rainy day, in a funeral attended only by a clutch of elderly party workers swathed in overcoats and huddling under a canopy of black umbrellas, and now he is buried not far from here, in a plot reserved for militant poets and thinkers, surrounded by his friends and foes, the poets of his generation, Bartini and Broides, Hanania Reichman, Dov Chomsky, Kamzon, Lichtenbaum and Maytos, Hanan Shadmi, Hanani, Akhai and Ukhmani.

> *Their love and their envy have faded away*
> *The pages are dust now and rusted their sword;*
> *The flowers in their garden are withered and gray —*
> *In silence they sleep and they praise not the Lord.*

Hallo, sorry, is that Lucy? Lucy? This is Ricky here. I don't suppose you remember me. Just a minute, I'll tell you where from. Just a moment. I'm sorry. You've got such a pretty voice still, Lucy, like the taste of red wine. I'm

Ricky — remember? Charlie's Ricky? From the thing with Charlie? You remember, Lucy? About fifteen years ago? I'm the Ricky that used to work at Isabella and Carmen's Beauty and Bridal Salon at the bottom of Allenby? Yes. It's me. Like, you and me was rivals then? Do you remember all that, Lucy? It's like even then I felt like I liked you even more than him? Like maybe I started going out with him just so I could, like, smell your smell on him? No, wait, Lucy, don't hang up, I swear, it's not what you think, believe me I'm the most normal human being in the whole world, just listen, give me two minutes. Never mind how I got hold of your number, with your new surname. I found it and that's that. Is it, like, your husband's name? Never mind. My fling with Charlie, do you remember? It took about a week, eight days maybe. Something like that. Barely. Then he went back to you. Crawled back, I should say. In any case, the whole thing with me was only because of you, Lucy, it only happened because you'd finished with him for a bit and specially because even then I was mad about you but I was too shy to tell you. Well, now, let's get to the point. It's like this. The reason I'm calling you is that maybe you feel like meeting up sometime, just the two of us, somewhere, we can sit and chat about all of that? And other things too? No, I don't mind where, you choose? But I'm paying? The coffee's on me? Tell me, Lucy, have you got a husband? Or somebody? Children? God forbid, I'm not giving you the third degree. Absolutely not. What gave you that idea? OK, Lucy, fine. Why not? Only don't think that I'm some kind of a psycho. It's like this. I often find myself thinking about you, Lucy, about your neck, your voice, your kind heart, your eyes, the mind you had in those days. A thousand times better than mine. It was as if you and me was on one side and Charlie was, well — believe me, I've already forgotten that Charlie. Why do we need to talk about him? Like, I've got nothing in common with him? Just with you, Lucy. Even though quite a few years have gone past, I haven't got over you. Listen, Lucy, this is how it is with me, just don't laugh at me, don't get the idea that I'm some poor bitch who's got nothing better to do with herself than to ring up someone from way back? No, don't take it like that. Try to take it, like, you and me, we're in the same boat? What do you mean, what do I mean in the same boat? Didn't Charlie chuck you the same way he chucked me? Used us and crumpled us up and threw us in the trash like an old Kleenex? OK, look, Lucy, we can't talk about this on the phone. Believe me, even though you must be thinking that I'm totally weird. Just a minute, Lucy, just a minute, don't hang up on me. Listen. It's like this: I'm not with anyone. Man or woman, if that's what you happen to be thinking. I've got nobody at all. Apart from you, I mean. Because often in my thoughts and even in my dreams in the middle of the night I imagine you and me together, Lucy? In a relationship? Partners? No, not what you're thinking, like, more like two sisters? You're probably thinking it's a bit wild? Totally wild, even? Aren't you? What, don't you ever think about

how the two of us, you and me, one week after the other,
one after the other, in the same hotel in Eilat, in the same
room, in the same king-size bed, how we both did it for
him at night and even in the middle of the day? We did,
like, exactly the same positions for him. First it was you
then a week later it was me and a week after that it was
you again? There were a whole lot of times when he called
me Lucy in the dark, once in broad daylight, in a sushi res-
taurant, and I was literally over the moon each time he
called me Lucy. I expect there were a whole lot of times in
the dark when he called you Ricky? No? And didn't he say
to you too sometimes suddenly, Come on, sweetie, give
me a goblet — you know what I mean — and do it as slow
as you can? Or, Come here, doll, let me tie you up a bit?
Or, Let me watch you peeing standing up? No? And then,
after he chucked me out and went back to you, and the
two of you went to the same hotel and the same room in
Eilat, don't tell me you never thought about me there? Just
a few times? Just thinking, like, that Ricky did exactly this
for him, and this? And maybe that? Didn't it ever cross
your mind that he must have taken that Ricky out to the
Las Vegas Bar and fed her from the spoon and tickled her
there under her skirt with the cocktail stick from the ol-
ive? Don't tell me you've never thought about the two of
us as though we were the same woman only split in two?
What do you say to the idea that we could go, the two of
us, to Eilat some day, let's say — take a room in the same
hotel? The same room even? Lucy, no, don't hang up on

me, I'm not nuts or anything, you've got to believe me, I'm just not, give me another couple of minutes? Lucy? Lucy?

Walking down an unfamiliar back street in the dark the Author collides with some barbed wire that has apparently been stretched across the pavement by children, between a No Parking sign and the railings of a fence. The wire was positioned at chest height and the Author, who has been walking briskly, lets out a short but angry cry of surprise, pain, and above all, of outrage: it is as though someone has slapped his face in the dark. Yet somehow he feels that the slap was not unexpected, that it was definitely deserved and has even made him feel a little better.

Surely Arnold Bartok, the gaunt, bespectacled man who lost his part-time job sorting parcels in a private courier firm a few days ago, could be found some work in the accountants' office where the Author is a partner: even something quite menial, in the mailroom or in maintenance. He could enjoy a small monthly wage, and in time, who knows, it may turn out that he is equipped for some other work, in accountancy or records. The Author himself is in charge of the tax affairs of four or five middle- to large-size export companies, particularly relating to their foreign-currency earnings. Arnold Bartok would surely turn out to be an obedient, grateful, and unobtrusive worker. But he wouldn't be able to curb his irritating tendency to make sarcastic remarks.

But what does Arnold Bartok do all day, now that he has lost his part-time job? How does he occupy himself in the long hours while his aged mother is snoring or reading novels in Hungarian?

Maybe he sits in a corner of the old laundry, at what used to be his father's ironing table, writing some private work about the possibility or otherwise of eternal life. One might say, he argues, that life and death came into the world together, as a dialectical pair whose members are indissolubly interdependent: say life and you've said death as well. And vice versa. The day life appeared on Earth, death appeared with it.

But this is a completely false supposition, Arnold Bartok reasons. For millions of years trillions of organisms flourished on Earth without any of them ever experiencing death. These single-cell organisms did not die, they divided themselves endlessly, one became two, two four, four eight, and so on. Death did not exist. Only in the present age, when a different form of reproduction, sexual reproduction, appeared, did ageing and death occur.

It follows that it is not life and death that came into the world as a pair but sex and death. And since death appeared later, eons later than life, it is surely possible to hope that it will vanish one day without life disappearing, too. Hence eternal life is a logical possibility. We simply have to find a way of eliminating sex, so as to rid our world of the inevitability of death, and of so much suffering as well.

On a small piece of paper Arnold Bartok draws a vertical line. To the right of it he writes the words: "Eternal life. Without suffering or humiliation." To the left of the line he writes: "Sex. Suffering. Decay. Ageing. Death." Then he writes underneath the two columns: "But the chances are very remote." And under these words he adds: "When was time created? What was there before time, what will there be afterwards? What good is time to us?" And right at the bottom: "The present condition is very bad."

The Author wonders whether he would have been capable of looking after his own mother, if she were still alive, as Arnold Bartok looks after old, paralyzed Ophelia who never stops ordering him around. The details of the physical relationship between mother and son — the sweat, the chamber pot, her bare, flabby buttocks, the wiping, the incontinence pad — fascinate the Author so powerfully that he screws up his face and feels the first waves of nausea. Hastily he moves his thoughts away from Arnold Bartok's invalid mother, from his own mother, and from eternal life, and resumes his meditation on Rochele Reznik's shyness.

After looking around and making sure there is no one in the street, the Author selects a narrow passage between two hedges and takes a long, leisurely piss. As he does so he thinks about Ovadya Hazzam who is dying of cancer in Ichilov Hospital, with a catheter fitted back into his urethra, slowly draining a cloudy fluid into a plastic container hanging by his bed and almost overflowing, but the night nurse is not at her station, she popped out a quarter of an hour ago to get herself a decaf from the adjoining ward, just on the other side of the elevators, but she is still there because she happened to bump into the cutest of the junior house doctors and she's chatting to him. Ovadya Hazzam, whose Buick these last few years has always been full of laughing blondes and who spent money left and right on good causes, politics, and having a good time, and even though he wore a little skullcap on his head that didn't stop him going away sometimes for the weekend to a casino in Turkey with a couple of Russian divorcees or maybe three, now has nobody to hear his groans. He calls out feebly several times to the nurse, who popped out for a moment twenty minutes ago. There is no one to respond to the emergency call button, but a hoarse voice shouts at him from the next bed, *Yallah,* cut it out, will you, people are trying to sleep here.

Thinking about Ovadya Hazzam, dying there in the hospital between two other dying men, both at least twenty years his senior, the Author zips up, returns to the avenue, taking care to avoid the barbed wire, and retraces his steps impatiently to the Shunia Shor and the Seven Victims of the Quarry Attack Cultural Center.

He thinks for a moment he can make out a shadowy form sitting on the steps of the cultural center, waiting for him, maybe that of Yuval Dahan or Dotan, the miserable young poet who apparently has not yet given up hope of intercepting the Author and is sitting, huddled and shivering, waiting for him to return, in the middle of the night, and sit beside him on the steps, and read at least four or five of his poems by the light of the street lamp, and then the two of them can have a heart-to-heart talk, till daybreak if need be, a totally open emotional and artistic exchange between a mature, experienced writer and a struggling novice beset by suffering and humiliation to the point of suicidal thoughts, and there is not a single soul in the whole wide world who can understand him except this Author, who has so often described such suffering in his books, and even though he is a famous celebrity I can read between the lines of his books enough to know that behind the well-known public persona there lurks someone shy and lonely and even possibly sad. Just like me. In fact, he and I are twin souls and that is why he is the only person who can understand me and maybe even help me because if he can't who can?

The building is locked and in darkness and in the entrance there are still notices announcing the literary event that concluded about two hours ago. The cultural administrator Yerucham Shdemati has left the light on in the ground-floor office to deter burglars.

But you would have to be a very naive burglar, a real beginner, the Author says to himself with a smile, to be put off by this light that is on night after night from evening to morning in an office that you can see into from the street to satisfy yourself that there is no one there. There is not a soul in the entire Shunia Shor and the Seven Victims of the Quarry Attack Cultural Center, apart perhaps from the shadowy figure of the boy poet shivering at the bottom of the steps, having given up all hope of your reading his poems or sitting and talking to him and asking nothing more of you than that you should notice his forlorn shadow, which may in fact be no more than the shadow of an empty packing case or a couple of broken benches. And remember his eyes, ridiculously enlarged behind his pebble glasses, and know that at this very moment, in the middle of the night, in the darkness of his bedroom which is not a real room but just a kitchen balcony closed off with plasterboard and some glass bricks in his parents' apartment on Reines Street, he is lying wide awake in the dark in his underwear, in a state of despair, thinking only of you.

Just across the road from the cultural center, in Rochele Reznik's rooftop room, if that is really the room she pointed out to him when they were standing here an hour or so ago, if he hasn't gotten confused, between her drawn curtains, a crack of light shows.

So, apparently she sent her curtains to some cleaning company that specializes in cleaning curtains after sunset and returning them to their owners beautifully washed and ironed before the stroke of midnight.

Unless you are mistaken, and her room is the other one up there? And in fact, the whole story of her curtains going to the cleaners' may just have been meant as a hint to you. A hint that you missed, that you shouldn't go up with her? Or the contrary, that you should? And you understood nothing and missed something that might have — or maybe you didn't miss it after all? After all, her light is still on.

And suddenly the Author enters the building, without asking himself why. He feels for the light button, taking great care this time in the dark, since one of his ribs still reminds him of the slap he got from the barbed wire earlier, and touching the place he finds that his shirt is torn in several places and that he is bleeding, and the blood on his fingers reminds him of forgotten schoolboy scraps.

Once he has managed to turn the light on in the stairwell, the Author pauses for a moment, as he always does, to examine the mailboxes at the foot of the stairs. Bilha and Shimon Perechodnik. The Arnon Family. Dr. Alphonse Valero, Structural Engineer. Yaniv Schlossberg. Rami & Tami Bentolila. Caplan, Accountants. Rochele and Joey Reznik. (In careful, rounded handwriting. Is "Joey" Joselito? Or has she got some lodger up there? Or even a partner? Perhaps?)

There is also a big box belonging to the tenants' council (ABSOLUTELY no circulars or handbills!!!). The stairwell is rather shabby, with peeling plaster and pencil scribbles, the banisters are rusting, the door of one of the meter cupboards hangs miraculously from a single bent hinge. Passing a door marked "Yaniv Schlossberg lives it up here," he hears a long salvo of bullets accompanied by whoops and cheers, and then the sound of breaking glass from the TV.

It's nearly midnight.

And you? What, may we ask, are you looking for here at this time of night? Are you entirely sane?

At this moment, hearing the sounds of shooting coming from Yaniv Schlossberg's apartment on the first floor, the Author decides that he ought to get out of here. His feet lead him of their own accord to the café where he sat earlier in the evening, the café with Ricky the waitress, the outline of whose underpants showed through her skirt.

Is the café still open? Is she perhaps sitting there all alone, at a corner table, sipping a last cup of hot chocolate before locking up? She's just about to go to the restroom and change from her skirt to jeans and a blouse and slip into some comfortable sandals, and when she leaves one could offer, for example, to walk her home to protect her from the kind of men who pester pretty, attractive girls like you in the empty streets at night?

Or maybe the Author does not leave when he reaches the first floor but persists in climbing up two more flights to Rochele Reznik's door. There he hesitates for a few moments, while the light on the stairs goes out, is relit by someone on a lower landing, and goes out again. The Author presses his ear to the door: is she still awake, or was the light he saw through the curtains merely a night-light that she keeps on when she is asleep? Is she alone with her cat? Or is there a hefty young lover sleeping by her side? Which would be profoundly embarrassing. How exactly do you see yourself right now, if you don't mind my asking? As the embodiment of the nocturnal desires of a lonely woman who is almost young, a nice, pleasant girl only not particularly attractive? Or do you cast yourself as the staircase rapist they've been searching for around here for more than eighteen months? Or simply as a confused and feverish man, like Yuval Dahan the young poet, who goes out looking for inspiration for a story in the middle of the night in dark stairwells?

> *Many a wise man lacks for sense,*
> *Etc., etc., etc.*

The devil now tempts our feverish Author to try the door gently. It's locked, of course.

So, what about your shy reader?

She went to sleep long ago, leaving her night-light on to attract muddled moths like you.

But there is another possibility. While he quietly lowers the door handle there is a sound from inside the apartment. At once he reconsiders and flees, too nervous to turn on the light on the stairs, taking them two at a time, losing his footing on the last bend, and bumping his shoulder violently on the door of the meter cupboard that was hanging miraculously by a single hinge and has now come loose and hits the banister railings with a tremendous crash, a door opens, probably that of "Yaniv Schlossberg lives it up here," Excuse me, would you mind telling me who you are looking for at this time of night?

Maybe he will recognize him? From pictures in the papers, or from chat shows on TV? And how can he explain? I'm sorry, I'm Mr. Hyde, would you mind letting me ring Dr. Jekyll urgently?

But it is also possible that the Author does not run away when he hears the sound inside the apartment but stays rooted to the spot, in paralyzed silence, outside Rochele Reznik's door. After a few moments he decides to leave a note for her, tucked between the door and the doorpost (or would it be better to leave it downstairs, in the mailbox she shares with Joselito?). This is what the note will say: You were magnificent this evening, Rochele, and I came back later on to thank you and also to be certain that you got back safely to your ivory tower and did not fall into the hands of any witch or dragon. And, if you'll permit me, this note is also to give you a goodnight kiss. (He will sign the note only with his initial. Or better still, he won't sign it at all — what's the point?)

Or perhaps this: just at the moment when the Author turns to flee, Rochele opens the door because she was not asleep, she was sitting on her bed, deep in thought, and she noticed the slight movement of the door handle in the middle of the night, and despite her panic she hurried over to look through the peephole, and when she saw who was there she did not hesitate or wait for him to knock but opened the door at once.

Rochele, wearing a plain short-sleeved cotton nightdress that reaches almost down to her ankles, buttoned all the way up to her neck. Did she manage to do up the two top buttons while she was peering through the peephole? Or is this the way she always sleeps, with her nightgown buttoned up to the top to protect her against whoever may be planning to sneak into her dreams?

Rochele Reznik smiles in surprise, with flickers of fear and joy on her squirrel face.

It's you? You've come back?

The Author, for his part, is surprised to discover that her night smile is less shy and embarrassed than her rare smiles earlier in the evening. His own embarrassment is so great now that he tries to mumble something, to gain some time, to invent some story, explanation, or apology for her, and then turn tail and run.

His lips speak of their own accord: It's like this. Rochele. Look. I came back because I found I'd forgotten something. I mean, I'd forgotten something I really wanted to do for you before. And I didn't do it. See if you can guess. What was it I forgot to do for you?

She stands beside the door, that she has hastily closed and locked behind him, with her arms firmly crossed over her chest as a barrier, or to hide its flatness under her nightdress. Her voice is quite calm now (perhaps because her embarrassment level has fallen as his has risen, like some experiment in physics): I give up. What was it you wanted to do and forgot?

Will you hand me your book for a moment?

My book? What book?

Your book. I mean my book. The one you read from this evening at the cultural center, which you read from so beautifully. I just wanted to write a few words in it, a little message for you, but I was so excited I forgot. It was only just now, half an hour ago, that I remembered. So I turned round and came straight back to you.

From the top of the bookcase a black-and-white cat eyes him with a haughty look, and winks ironically, as though there's nothing novel about this visitor, as though this is the usual pattern of life up here under the roof, every night, at midnight, some writer or other always turns up, blushing, after remembering to come and write a personal message to Rochele Reznik on the flyleaf of his latest book.

Pleased to meet you. You must be Mister Joey? The Author advances, uninvited, into the middle of the room, to the bedside table, where he bends over and writes her a warm dedication, adding the name of jealous Joselito, then he bends over again and adds a drawing of a little flower and a bewhiskered cat's face that, for some reason, looks crafty and scheming.

Rochele says: Listen. I must apologize to you. I was wrong. When you brought me home I told you my curtains were at the cleaners'. And they weren't.

And a moment later: No. Actually it's not that I was wrong, but I didn't tell you the truth. I'm sorry.

Why did you do that? Was it because you were looking

for an excuse to stop me from coming upstairs? Were you a bit frightened? (His hand flutters for a moment, absent-mindedly, above her cheek. Not pityingly, or seductively, but something like late-night affection.)

Yes. I was frightened. I don't know. I felt shy with you. I honestly can't say now if I really wanted you to come up but I was afraid, or if I was afraid to say to you simply, listen, it's better if you don't come up, or if I was afraid to say I was afraid. I don't even know now.

Hearing these words he draws her head toward him, presses her to his shoulder and holds her tight, so she can't escape. (Little frightened squirrel, please don't run away from me.) Meanwhile he notices that now, maybe because she has untied her plait for the night and her thick long hair is streaming halfway down her back, she is suddenly looking much less unattractive.

And like a shy girl, as his hand presses her head to his shoulder, she suddenly utters an unexpected question: Just now, I said, I don't even know now. Shouldn't I have said, Even now I don't know?

Hugging her shoulders he leans her back against the table and kisses her under the ear, an ambiguous, more or less paternal, kiss. But still he cannot stop the flow of his own words:

Well, let's see. You don't even know now? Now you don't even know? Even now you don't know? Now you even don't know? Now even you don't know? No, do you even know now? Please cross out those that do not apply.

Instead of which her lips tickle his neck, barely touching his skin, and only then does the Author finally realize that he should stop talking. So he abandons his wordplay and feels embarrassed about the bristles that must have grown since he shaved this morning and may be scratching her. But the bristles seem to inspire her to scrape the back of his neck with her fingernails, not gently this time but with a sudden force. In response, he turns her round so she has her back to him, draws her hair aside, rests his lips on the nape of her neck, and moves his tongue lightly back and forth over the fine hairs until they stiffen, and ripples run down her back. Then he turns her again and kisses her lips cautiously, tentatively, and at once the kiss becomes deeper, their tongues moving back and forth, kisses that simultaneously quench and excite the appetite. He breathes in her smells, among which he thinks he can make out a faint smell of mouthwash with an almost imperceptible hint of lemon-flavored yogurt and bread. This cocktail of smells enchants and excites him more than any perfume in the world. For one fleeting moment he is worried about his own body odor and the smell that may be coming from his own mouth, and regrets not asking if he can take a shower first, but how could he have done that? And now it is too late to ask her anything because she has started pressing herself against him and seeking out his chest with her lips, with a certain shyness yet with an urgency or passion that overcomes her shyness and sweeps away her inhibitions, as though her own body is driving her along and begging her not to hold it back.

Now that she is pressing herself passionately against

him he is anxious that she will be repelled or alarmed or even offended when she suddenly feels his erection through their clothes. But when she does discover it, far from being upset or repelled, as though her solitary dreams have prepared her for this moment, she holds him tight and squeezes her body to his, sending delightful sailing boats tacking to and fro across the ocean of his back. With her fingertips she sends foam-flecked waves scurrying over his skin.

Standing beside her single bed, it is not difficult for them to move from the vertical to the horizontal and soon they find themselves lying together on their sides (because the bed is so narrow). Just then something indescribable happens, a simple movement intended to make them more comfortable, a movement that they both happen to make at the very same moment, that they both happen to make in perfect harmony, like a pair of dancers bringing off a precisely synchronized move after a hundred rehearsals, and this wonderful, unimaginably perfect movement makes them both giggle and thus removes any lingering embarrassment or tension from their path while heightening their excitement. And because the bed is so narrow they have to go on lying on their sides holding each other tight and they somehow have to coordinate each move, like a pas de deux. And apart from a single meeting between an elbow and a shoulder the dance is perfectly fluid, which amazes him because he imagined that she was not particularly experienced and he does not consider himself exactly a virtuoso. When his hand moves down to her thigh she whispers: Just a moment, let me go and shut Joselito in the shower, he makes me feel awkward. And he whispers back: Let him watch us, who cares if he gets jealous? He may pick up a trick or two.

He hears her talking to the cat in a warm, affectionate voice, before she shuts the bathroom door. Then she is back in bed, lying on her side, holding and stroking him, neither of them sure what to do next, until his fingers stray over her breasts through the cotton nightdress, and she enfolds his hand in hers and guides it away from her small breasts that have always caused her embarrassment, and as though to compensate him she moves it down to rest on her belly.

Recovering the urge to speak he says in a muffled voice, Listen, Rochele, but he gives up when she stops his lips. Instead he kisses her forehead, her temples, the corners of her eyes, beneath her ears, in the hollows of her neck, where it curves down to meet her shoulders, and where the touch of his lips tickles her slightly. These kisses are designed to bribe her or distract her attention from the slow, stealthy progress of his hand, which does not rest on her belly where it has been placed but is creeping steadily southward. But Rochele stops him: Wait for me a moment, she says, I'm still a bit scared. And he stops obediently and whispers: You'll be surprised, little squirrel, but I'm a bit scared myself. It's not just you.

And even though he does not consider that there is the

slightest resemblance between her shy apprehension and his own fear of failure, in fact the two fears are rather similar. She probably sees him as an experienced lover who is bound to find whatever her untaught body can offer him disappointingly bland, while he, as usual, is afraid that his desire will abandon him without prior warning, as has already happened to him several times, and then what will she think of him? Or of herself? What will she make of him bursting into her home at midnight, full of passion, only for it to turn out that his ardor was no more than posturing and deception? What will she think when she finds out that the man she imagined to be skilled and practiced is actually no more virile than an overexcited youngster liable to shrivel up completely?

And indeed, no sooner does this fear enter his mind than it becomes a reality. After holding her tightly to him now he has to ease her body away to prevent her noticing what is missing.

Just a moment ago he was worried that she might become aware of his erection; now he has the opposite anxiety, that she may become aware of its absence.

A mischievous little imp scampers into his thoughts and points out to him that now they are quits: she has been taking care all along not to press her breasts against you, so that you won't notice how small they are, while now you are withdrawing your loins from her for more or less the same reason.

Should he whisper to her what the imp just told him?

They could enjoy a liberating laugh together, which will relieve their anxieties and they will be left with no more worries or guilty secrets, nothing ridiculous or awkward, and then they can really start enjoying themselves.

But instead he hastens to silence the little gremlin and says nothing. Instead of whispering a comparison that is no comparison at all he starts kissing her shoulders, her flank, tactfully skirting her breasts but stooping to nibble at her tummy, and on the way, between kisses, he gives her a few skillful caresses that draw out from deep inside her a soft gurgling sound, like a low, long-drawn-out cooing.

While he caresses Rochele he closes his eyes tight and tries to recover lost ground by visualizing the outline of Ricky's underwear, the asymmetric line of her underpants that was visible through her short skirt and caused him so much excitement earlier in the evening, before the literary event. He forces himself to imagine Ricky lifting her skirt up to her hips for him with one hand while slipping the other into her underpants and pulling them open at the crotch. And he also conjures up detailed pictures of what must have taken place in the hotel room in Eilat between this same Ricky and her footballer lover, Charlie, or between Charlie and Lucy, runner-up in the Queen of the Waves contest, in the same room in the same hotel, or what might have taken place between Charlie and the two girls together, or between Ricky and Lucy in bed together on their own, without Charlie.

And when none of this helps him, he asks his imagination to transform him for a few minutes into Yuval, the young poet who hungers so much for a woman's body day and night that he despises his own life: so now you are Yuval, and at last you've been given a nearly naked woman's body, take it, do what you like with it, strip off her nightie and quench all your feverish thirst.

Rochele notices, or maybe she just guesses, his alternating pride and humiliation. Burying her face in the cavity of his shoulder she says in her innermost voice: Tell me that you're really here? Come on, convince me that it's not all happening in a dream?

Maybe it is because she believes it is all happening in a dream that she does not stop his hand when it raises the hem of her nightdress above her hips. Not only does she not stop him, she takes his hand and guides it to another texture that feels finer and far silkier than that of her nightdress, a warm texture that discloses hints of folds and moist recesses to his touch, until he swells once more and has no need of poor Yuval or Ricky the waitress or the outline of her panties under her skirt. Almost in an instant his desire rises to a level where the pressure to reach a climax stalls and gives way to a sort of sensitive physical alertness, pleased with its own sexual generosity, that gets a kick out of giving her thrill after thrill and postponing his own satisfaction, feeling to see how he can give her more and more pleasure, until she cannot take any more. And so, in complete self-denial — in every sense — with his fingers, now experienced and even inspired, he starts to steer her enjoyment like a ship toward its home port, to the deepest anchorage, right to the core of her pleasure.

Attentive to the very faintest of signals, like some piece of sonar equipment that can detect sounds in the deep imperceptible to the human ear, he registers the flow of tiny moans that rise from inside her as he continues to excite her, receiving and unconsciously classifying the fine nuances that differentiate one moan from another, in his skin rather than in his ears he feels the minute variations in her breathing, he feels the ripples in her skin, as though he has been transformed into a delicate seismograph that intercepts and instantly deciphers her body's reactions, translating what he has discovered into skillful, precise navigation, anticipating and cautiously avoiding every sandbank, steering clear of each underwater reef, smoothing any roughness except that slow roughness that comes and goes and comes and turns and goes and comes and strokes and goes and makes her whole body quiver. Meanwhile her moaning has turned into little sobs and sighs and cries of surprise, and suddenly his lips tell him that her cheeks are covered in tears. Every sound, every breath or shudder, every wave passing over her skin, helps his fingers on their artful way to steer her home.

And the higher the waves of her pleasure, the more his own pride swells, and the more he enjoys postponing his own satisfaction, delaying it until her stifled sobs are all released — until the rising flood sweeps her like a paper boat over the rapids. (Despite his noble aspirations, and for all his devotion to duty, from time to time he does snatch a hasty earnest of pleasures to come by rubbing his tense body along her thigh with a friction that slakes and yet sharpens his lust — before focusing once more on his precise and self-imposed steering.)

Like a musician now, totally absorbed in the movement of his fingertips over the keys, he no longer recalls how just a few hours earlier he found this shy squirrel pleasant and almost pretty but not attractive. His hands are drawn to discover her breasts, the breasts of a twelve-year-old girl, under her nightgown, and this time she does not stop him, immersed as she is in her own pleasure; and when he cups them in his hands he is filled with compassion and desire and brings his tongue to her nipples and takes each nipple in turn between his lips, delicately courting them with his tongue, while his fingers play on her labia and the secret petals around a bud so full and firm it almost resembles a third nipple. His lips and tongue follow his fingers' lead. And she, like a baby, suddenly thrusts her thumb into her mouth and begins sucking on it loudly, until her back suddenly arches like a stretched bow, and a moment later, when she has sunk back onto the mattress, a long, soft cry bursts as though from the bottom of the sea, expressing not only pleasure but astonishment, as though it were the first time in her life she had reached that landing stage, as if even in her wildest dreams she never imagined what was waiting for her here.

And suddenly she starts to weep aloud, and says to him, Look, I'm crying. And this girlish weeping makes her bury her little rodent's face in his shoulder and whisper: I'm sorry, it's just that I'm still a little bit shy with you.

She starts stroking him on his cheek and his brow, long, slow caresses that silence her weeping and calm her down. But two or three minutes later she suddenly sits up in bed and raises her arms in the air as she pulls her cotton nightdress, which was rolled up round her hips, over her head, now hidden from view for a moment, and she says, Now I don't care if you see me. And she lies down on her back again, open and waiting for him. But he merely lies on his side, in a fetal position, so as to hide the failure that overtook him the moment she relaxed after her own pleasure. He fears she may be upset by it, or that she may blame herself.

But she, summoning up courage she had no idea she was capable of, surprises herself and him by wetting her fingers and reaching out hesitantly to his penis. To and fro she slides her fingers in a moist caress such as she never dared administer either to her first boyfriend when she was young, twelve years ago, or to the married man five and a half years later.

This caress reveals to her what she has already guessed, and far from being upset she is swept by a wave of affection, generosity and motherly compassion at his discomfiture, his anxieties and his shame at what she must be thinking.

Stirred by a feminine resolve accompanied by a feeling that she must do whatever she can to help him, she overcomes her own inhibition and licks her fingers, closes them round his limp member and rolls it around in a hesitant movement that, despite her inexperience, is so rich in dedication, enthusiasm, and tenderness that it seems almost devotional, as though her hand were anointed with myrrh. With her five ambition-filled fingers she diligently works on him, over and over again, not exactly knowing but attempting to guess accurately, and then with her lips, with the velvet of her tongue, persistently, like an assiduous schoolgirl, until the first jerks begin to announce that he will soon hold his head up high.

At that precise moment he remembers the man who sat all through the evening in a corner of the hall releasing periodic chuckles and sniggers, Arnold, Arnold Bartok, a thin, gaunt, slightly shrunken man, a sick monkey that has lost most of its fur, only a month or so ago he was fired from his part-time job sorting parcels in a private courier company, and he and his invalid mother spend these sweaty nights in a former laundry, under the same sheet, and every hour or two he has to push a chamber pot under her flabby body and then remove it. Arnold Bartok, who is interested in eternal life and in the possibility of eliminating death.

This thought kills off any remaining glimmer of desire. Rochele's devoted fingers are unable to eliminate what Arnold Bartok is doing to him, perhaps by way of belated revenge. The young poet Yuval also appears in his thoughts, patiently standing and waiting his turn in the line of autograph hunters, not to have his copy of the book signed but to tell the Author, less in anger than in extremely low spirits: You wronged me a little, didn't you?

The Author attempts vainly to explain to Rochele what has no explanation. Even a more experienced woman might have become confused and even blamed herself for failing.

He, for his part, hastily accepts responsibility both for his limp state and for the distress he has caused her.

If only it were possible to put it into words, even in a whisper in bed in the dark, close to two o'clock in the morning, Rochele might, he thinks, find the courage to say something like this: Don't be sad, I beg of you, don't be sad, even a tiny bit, and don't apologize at all, there's no need, because your limp penis is penetrating me, right now, yes, penetrating me and reaching deep inside me, reaching places that no stiff penis has ever reached in my life and where no stiff penis could ever reach, so deep inside.

But how could she express such a feeling, aloud or in a whisper, to a man she hardly knows except from reading his books?

By the pale light of the street lamp filtering in through the crack between her curtains, she gets out of bed. She feels for her nightdress on the floor and picks it up. She shuts herself in the bathroom and emerges ten minutes later clean, fresh and fragrant, wearing another nightdress as long as the first one, reaching down to her ankles. Both its buttons are done up, too. She also frees Joselito, the devil in cat's clothing, and he wastes no time in regaining his lookout post close to the ceiling, on the top shelf of the bookcase, from where his yellow panther's eyes gleam down, hostile, curious or empty of any emotion, at the stranger who has usurped his place in the bed, as if to say, So, why did you bother? Or, I knew it would end like this, and so did you, by the way.

The stranger lies wretchedly on his back, smoking a cigarette, feeling a brutish male shame and also embarrassed to experience this age-old failure which makes him feel like a bull or a stallion that has proved unequal to its task, yet comforting himself with a mute pride over the pleasure he has given Rochele and the diapason of sighs and groans he has extracted from her. At once he feels ashamed at the arrogance of this self-congratulation. If only he could say to her, Listen, Rochele, please don't be sad, after all, the characters in this book are all just the Author himself: Ricky, Charlie, Lucy, Mr. Leon, Ovadya, Yuval, Yerucham, they are all just the Author and whatever happens to them here is really only happening to him, and even you, Rochele, are just a thought in my mind and whatever is happening to you and me is actually only happening to me.

But look, she says, you've got a scratch here, quite a deep one. You've even been bleeding. Can I disinfect it for you, and put a plaster on it?

Leave it, it's nothing.

Did you bump into something? Your shirt is torn.

I fought a dragon for you. I fought against seven wizards, five demons, and a dragon. I slew them all for you, but first they cut me with a sword.

Keep still. Don't be frightened, it's only iodine. It'll just sting for a moment. That's it, all done. How come you slay wizards and dragons and you're scared of a drop of iodine and a sticky plaster?

Now here he is, no longer lying on his back, no longer ashamed or triumphant, because now he is busy: he gets up, wraps himself in her sheet, lights another cigarette, stubs it out after taking a few puffs, gathers up his scattered clothing, goes into the bathroom to have a pee and a shower — in cold water — and emerges dressed but soaked because he decided not to dry himself: it's more refreshing.

Coffee? A roll? Toast? It won't take five minutes.

No thanks, little squirrel, I'm off. It's almost half past two.

Wait. The water's boiling. Have a coffee at least.

No thank you, forgive me but I really and truly have to run. ("Really," "really and truly," those code words which barely conceal a lie.)

Tell me, it was good, wasn't it?

Very. I had a wonderful time with you. And listen. Rochele. I'll ring you soon. (You won't ring. Why should you?) And try not to be angry. With me or with yourself.

And don't be sad. (But she's already sad, because of you, wretch, and you know she is, as you knew she would be.) So, see you? Bye, Joselito, and I'm warning you, take good care of this young lady, otherwise you'll have me to reckon with. (It is getting harder for him to disguise his impatience. His hand is already on the door handle, the same handle that he tried very cautiously from the outside less than three hours ago, although in fact he preferred then that the door should stay locked. But in that case, why did you come up here? Why did you try the handle?)

Wait a minute. How about an herbal tea, at least? I've got some yerba mate from Argentina, too. Why don't you stay the night? We're inviting you, aren't we, Joselito?

Thank you both, really, but I really do have to go. I'll ring you. We'll talk.

And her voice is suddenly low and quivering again, as it was when they first came out of the cultural center: Are you disappointed? With me?

Disappointed? Why should I be? What about?

She says nothing. Her fingers try to button up her nightdress, but they fail because it is already buttoned.

No. Not disappointed. Why? You were wonderful, Rochele. (But these are hollow words, because he is already asking himself what on earth brought him here in the middle of the night. What got into him? His hand is already on the door handle, and he is glancing at his watch: he's been here for two and a half hours. A little more: two hours and forty minutes.)

I just want you to know that I —

I know, Rochele. (He interrupted her on purpose, so as not to hear what she was apparently about to say.) I know. And don't worry. After all, you yourself said that we had a truly wonderful time together. Well, I'll be seeing you. Go back to sleep till the morning. Or till midday, why not? (The words "after all," "why not," and particularly the word "truly," make his empty speech even more hollow and false. Shabby, he says to himself. Shameful, he says to himself.)

What next? Maybe go to check if Ricky's café is still open at twenty past two in the morning, and if by any chance Ricky herself is still there?

So here he is out in the dark again, dragging his feet from the street to the avenue and from the avenue to one side street after another. Well, where have you been? His penis is starting to give signs of life all of a sudden. Welcome back, you dummy. Do you remember what you missed? I'm very sorry, but which of us do you think is the bigger idiot, you or me? So just you shut up.

As he crosses an empty street lit by yellow street lamps and turns right into an empty, almost dark side street, the Author starts mentally sketching in some more lines in the character of Mrs. Miriam Nehorait and that of Yerucham Shdemati, the cultural administrator, so they don't come out flat.

Meanwhile his feet have led him to an unfamiliar

neighborhood, not far from the point where the city ends and the empty night fields begin.

> *The wind blows where it listeth,*
> *And as it blows it sings:*
> *Perchance this time the soaring wind*
> *Will lift you on its wings.*

Next to an unfinished building stands a thickset, slightly hunchbacked night watchman, lifting one shoulder while he takes a long, motionless piss. Behind him is nothing but a row of electricity pylons, an unmade pavement, some sheds, corrugated-iron shelters, piles of sand and gravel. The street tails off into a dirt track, and here is the end of the city: fields of thistles, four rusty barrels, empty building plots piled high with rubble, broken furniture, shadowy castor-oil plants on the slope, the skeleton of a jeep, a tire half buried in the sand, at last you are alone. You sit down on an upturned crate. You see the dim outlines of hills. Stars. Flickering lights in windows. A witless traffic light changing color aimlessly, amber, red, green. Barking of distant dogs and a faint smell of sewage. Why write about all these things? They exist, and will go on existing whether you write about them or not, whether you are here or not. Surely these are the basic questions that figured at the beginning of this text: Why do you write? Why do you write the way you do? What contribution do your books make to society, to the State, or to the enhancement of moral values? Whom do you hope to influence? Do you actually only write for the fame? Or for the money?

When he was sixteen or seventeen, the age that the young poet Yuval Dotan is now, the Author used to sit alone at night in an abandoned storeroom where he poured out fragments of muddled stories onto paper. He wrote more or less the same way as he dreamed or masturbated: a mixture of compulsion, enthusiasm, despair, disgust, and wretchedness. And in those days he also had an insatiable curiosity to try to understand why people hurt each other, and themselves, without meaning to at all.

Nowadays he is still curious to understand, but over the years he has gradually acquired a physical dread of bodily contact with strangers: even a slight accidental contact terrifies him. Even the touch of a stranger's hand on his shoulder. Even the need to inhale air that may have been in other people's lungs. And yet he continues to watch them and write about them so as to touch them without touching, and so that they touch him without really touching him.

One could put it like this: he writes about them as if he were a photographer from the days of sepia photographs, taking a group portrait. He runs around among the sitters, chatting to them all, making friends, joking, instructing them to settle down and take their places, arranging them in a semicircle, with the men standing at the back, the shorter ones with the women and children sitting in front, closing up the gaps, moving heads closer together, walking among them two or three times, straightening a collar here, a sleeve there, or a hair ribbon, then retreating behind the camera perched on its tripod, burying his head in the black cloth, closing one eye, counting aloud one-two-three, finally pressing the trigger and turning them all into ghosts. (Only Miriam Nehorait's gray cat refused to be still, maybe he sniffed the presence of Joselito, so he has been immortalized in a corner of the picture with three or four tails. Lisaveta Kunitsin blinked and looks as though she is winking. The bald pate of Mr. Leon, the gangster's hench-man, reflects an unhealthy glow. The young poet Yuval Da-han/Dotan forgot to smile, but Charlie is grinning broadly, Rochele Reznik is looking down at the tips of her shoes, while Lucy, runner-up in the Queen of the Waves contest, has a slight, not unattractive squint in her left eye.)

But why write about things that exist even without you? Why describe in words things that are not words?

Moreover, what purpose, if any, is served by your sto-ries? Whom do they benefit? Who, if you will excuse the question, needs your shabby fantasies about all kinds of worn-out sex scenes with frustrated waitresses, lonely readers who live with cats, or runners-up in Eilat Queen of the Waves contests from years ago? Maybe you wouldn't mind explaining to us, please, briefly and in your own words, what the Author is trying to tell us here?

He is covered in shame and confusion because he ob-serves them all from a distance, from the wings, as if they all exist only for him to make use of in his books. And with the shame comes a profound sadness that he is always an outsider, unable to touch or to be touched, with his head perpetually buried under the photographer's old black cloth.

You cannot write without looking behind you; like Lot's wife. And in doing so you turn yourself and them into blocks of salt.

To write about things that exist, to try to capture a color or smell or sound in words, is a little like playing Schubert when Schubert is sitting in the hall, and perhaps sniggering in the darkness.

> *It's green and peaceful here, a crow*
> *stands on a pillar, all alone,*
> *a pair of cypress trees together*
> *and another on its own.*

You need to make a correction. Your description of Mrs. Miriam Nehorait was not entirely accurate: swollen legs with purple varicose veins and a wizened face wrapped in cultural sweetness. Later, when she came up to you, you noticed her delicate mouth, her well-shaped fingers, her pleasant brown eyes, like those of an enthusiastic child, with long, gently upturned lashes. Twice every day she feeds eight alley-cats, one of which is missing an ear. Yechiel Nehorai, her husband, was run over nine years ago when he was a Zionist emissary in Montevideo. Her two married sons are both gynecologists in New York. (One of them is married to the daughter of the peeping neighbor, the optician Lisaveta Kunitsin.)

For some time now a hesitant, ill-defined relationship has been developing between Miriam Nehorait, a mature woman who has lived on her own for years in a two-room apartment with a little entrance hall, and her widowed neighbor, Yerucham Shdemati, the bubbly cultural administrator, with his noisy gaiety and his body odor, the man whose face looks like an old loaf of bread that has stood for too long in the basket and has started to shrivel and crack. Once, in the sixties, he was put thirteenth on the Labor Union Zionist Workers' Party list, and he was nearly elected to the Knesset. He was one of the last remaining campaigners for the creation of a general commune of all the workers in the Land of Israel, Jews and Arabs, men and women, who would all work to the best of their ability and put their monthly earnings into the communal chest, from which each worker would be paid a standard basic wage, with supplements according to the number of children, the state of health and the educational and cultural needs of each working family, according to the condition and the real needs of each. He believes that people are by nature generous and that it is only social pressures that drive us all into the arms of selfishness, greed, and exploitation. This evening, before you both went up onto the dais, he asked you to remind him later to tell you something about Rabbi Alter Druyanov's *Book of Jokes and Witticisms.* You forgot to remind him, and now it's too late. So now you will never know the key difference between a joke and a witticism. You are unlikely to meet Yerucham Shdemati again.

You ought to pause here for a moment, to take the time to give this character some habits that will fix him in your readers' memory, two or three significant eccentricities. For example, his habit of lustily licking the gummed strip on the back of an envelope with the whole width of his tongue, as though it were some kind of sweet. Yerucham Shdemati also licks stamps with a great abundance of saliva, with sensual greed, after which he likes to stick them on the envelope with a mighty thump of the fist, which makes Miriam Nehorait, who is fascinated by his "latent Tartar side," jump out of her skin.

He always answers the telephone at the first ring, with a broad, expansive gesture as though he were throwing a stone, and shouts into the receiver: Yes, Shdemati here, who is calling please? Bartok? No, I don't know any Bartok, Arnold or not Arnold, no, my dear comrade, absolutely not, on no account, I'm sorry but I am not authorized to divulge the Author's telephone number, I have not received the necessary permission, very sorry, comrade, why, if you don't mind my asking, don't you try to get it from the Writers' Union, for example? Huh?

Yerucham Shdemati almost always has bruises on his elbows or his forehead or his shoulder or his knee — a result of his fixed habit of ignoring inanimate objects and trying to walk straight through them as though they were made of air. Or maybe it is the opposite, and the inanimate objects bear a grudge and conspire against him. At any moment a chair back may butt him, the corner of the bathroom cabinet collide with his forehead, or a slice of bread spread with honey lies in wait for him on the bench just where he is about to sit down, the cat's tail plants itself right underneath the sole of his shoe and a glass of boiling hot tea hankers after his trousers. He also still composes furious letters to the editor of the evening paper denouncing some injustice or pitilessly exposing the ugliness, the arrogance, the ignominy, and the lies that have infected politics in particular and society in general in this country of ours.

In the morning he stands for a long time, sweaty and solidly built in his pajama trousers and a yellowing undershirt, at the basin in his bathroom, never closing the door as he performs his thorough, noisy ablutions, and with legs outspread he leans over the basin, washing and scrubbing his face, the back of his neck, his broad shoulders, his chest covered in white curls, snorting and gargling under the running tap, shaking his wet head from side to side like a dog that has been in water, squeezing each nostril in turn and emptying its contents into the basin, clearing his throat and hawking so noisily that Miriam Nehorait, who is on the other side of the wall in her own kitchen, is alarmed. Then he stands there for another three minutes toweling himself dry energetically, as though he were scrubbing a frying pan.

If, however, somebody praises an omelet he has made, a picture on his wall, the achievements of the early pioneers, the dock strike in Haifa, or the beauty of the sunset outside his window, his eyes moisten in gratitude.

Underneath his inflamed discourse on every subject under the sun, from the decline in the status of workers to the general infantilization of culture in Israel and worldwide, there is a constantly gushing geyser of jollity, a Gulf Stream of cheery warmth and kindheartedness. Even when he tries to raise his voice threateningly and burst into a wounded roar, his face still beams optimistically with a tireless enthusiasm.

Yerucham Shdemati always greets his brother's granddaughter with a fixed riddle or joke: Tell me, my little *krasavitsa*, what is it that goes around with its baby in its pocket? Is it a kangaroo? Or is it a can'tgaroo? Or maybe it's a shan'tgaroo? Which is it? Hee-hee! (He completely overlooks the fact that his great-niece is no longer a small child, in fact she's fourteen and a half.) So as to maintain this outward appearance of being jolly, dynamic, and positive (in the trade-unionist sense of the term), Yerucham Shdemati hides both from his great-niece and from Miriam Nehorait the fact that he is suffering from a blood disease from which, according to his brother the doctor, his chances of recovery are remote.

By now it is three o'clock in the morning. And there may be another correction to make, the Author says to himself as he crosses an empty street on the red light, peering to left and right and seeing that there is no one around and that the single street lamp is flickering as though wondering if there is any point. I could, for example (let's say, at nine o'clock tomorrow morning) bring Charlie — Charlie who was once the reserve goalkeeper of Bnei-Yehuda football team, he was the boyfriend of Lucy, the runner-up in the Queen of the Waves contest, then he was the boyfriend of Ricky, the waitress, then he was Lucy's boyfriend again, and he spent a delicious week with each of them at his uncle's hotel in Eilat, and now he has a family and a factory in Holon manufacturing solar water heaters that he even exports to Cyprus — at nine o'clock tomorrow morning I could bring him to Ichilov Hospital for a surprise visit to Ovadya Hazzam.

But why should he come alone? He'll be scared to come on his own. The phrase "terminally ill" terrifies him. Better for him to come with his wife. No, not his wife: let him come with Lucy, his friend from the good old days, the one he used to call affectionately Gogog.

Not with Lucy. With Ricky. This morning you can see through her summer blouse that she isn't wearing a bra, and you can see two dark puppy dogs that nuzzle her blouse with every step. Charlie used to call her Gogog, too.

In fact, why doesn't Charlie come with both of them?

Ovadya Hazzam opens his eyes suddenly and tries to wave his hand. He is too weak, and the skeletal hand falls back on the sheet, and he murmurs, Why have you come, honestly, you didn't have to. Then he murmurs something else but so faintly that Charlie and the girls can't understand. The patient in the next bed has to translate for them: He wants you to bring some chairs from over there by the window. He just wants you to sit down.

Charlie is suddenly smitten with fear mixed with pity and a slight disgust and shame for the disgust, and he tries to talk cheerfully, too loudly, as though the man who is dying of cancer is also suffering from partial deafness. Well, it's like this. He's come with the two girls to get Ovadya out of here. *Yallah,* Charlie shouts kindheartedly, come on, you old poseur, you've been cooped up here long enough, come out for a bit, we'll show you off out there like a young lion, we'll have the party to end all parties. Here, lean on these two cuties I've brought you, and off we go. What were you thinking, that we'd just come to visit? Nah, we didn't come to visit, we came to get you outta here. The girls will dress you and you'll soon be out, and meantime you can decide which one of the two you prefer, compliments of Charlie, or maybe you'd like to have the two of them? For you — the two of them, on the house.

Again the invalid murmurs a few hoarse words, and Charlie says, What, what, can't hear, speak clearly, and again the patient in the next bed translates: He's saying Charlie's Angels. He's talking about your girls. He means, like in the TV series *Charlie's Angels.* He means it as a joke.

While he is chatting to Ovadya Hazzam and the patient in the next bed, Charlie suddenly grasps that Ovadya Hazzam is really going to die. Before he came he was told that his condition was pretty serious, but he thought that "serious" meant something like a smashed knee or six broken ribs. Now he suddenly realizes that for the first time in his life he is touching a dying man, and the discovery fills him with panic and also with a wild joy that thank God the man who's dying is somebody else and not himself, that he's strong and healthy and will walk out of here in a minute whereas Ovadya isn't going anywhere. Ever.

Charlie feels so ashamed of this feeling that he raises his voice even more and jokes so much that the dying man makes a gesture and mutters something that Charlie can't hear and even the patient in the next bed has trouble hearing, and Ovadya Hazzam has to repeat it over and over again before the neighbor manages to translate: Orangeade. He said orangeade. He's thirsty, he wants a bottle of orangeade.

Orangeade, Charlie wonders, where on earth can we find orangeade? They stopped making it a hundred years ago. Well, twenty at least. Lucy? Ricky? Orangeade? When was the last time you saw such a thing?

The patient next door insists vindictively: That's what he's asking for. That's the only thing he wants. Nothing else will do. What are you going to do for him?

Charlie scratches the back of his neck and continues the movement by patting Ricky on the head.

Yallah, my lovelies, can't you see our friend here is feeling low? So why don't you cheer him up a bit. The two of you, together: start stroking his head and his body. Take away the pains. Haven't you got eyes in your heads? Can't you see our friend is in pain? So show him everything you've learned from me. Go to it. Give him a good time. Gogog and Gogog. The two of you.

While he is talking, Charlie himself bends down, overcoming his fear and disgust, and begins to stroke the patient's sweaty head, his cheeks, his pale forehead, weeping as he does so, and begging the patient who has also started crying: That's enough, man, don't cry, you'll be fine, you'll see you'll be as right as rain, trust me, trust your old brother to get you out of here, go on, girls, you stroke him too, as if you mean it, stroke him with love and stop whining.

And so on, until the patient in the next bed, who also has tears in his eyes, rings for the nurse and gestures that enough is enough, the patient is getting overexcited, she should gently but firmly usher his visitors out.

What about Rochele Reznik? You promised her you'd ring her over the next few days, you'd definitely ring her, soon, absolutely, but you didn't get her number. Because you didn't ask her for it. You forgot to ask. Standing alone in her frugal, simply furnished room, with its clean smell, its light-colored curtains, wearing a chaste nightdress, by the light of a lamp with a macramé shade, carefully folding her clean underwear, having thrown her dirty nightdress and underwear in the laundry basket, she feels sad as she looks at her flat body in the mirror on the inside of her wardrobe door: If only I had my mother's breasts, or my sister's, my whole life would be different. Why didn't I let him come up? After all, he begged me, in his polite, fatherly way, to ask him in. I could have said, Come in. I could have made him some tea or yerba mate or even a snack. I could have told him, seeing that he liked the way I read, that I can also sing. I could even have sung to him. Or put on some music, while we drank tea or Argentinean yerba mate. And then the two of us might suddenly —

There can't be a girl in the world who says no to him, but I'm so spoilt —

And now I'll never never —

Now he probably thinks I'm weird. Unwomanly.

Just look, Joselito, look what a fool I am. I'm the biggest fool there's ever been. (She says these last words aloud, grinning but close to tears.)

In her buttoned-up nightdress, the plain cotton nightdress of a boarding-school girl in the old days, she now sits, thin and stiffly upright, on the edge of her bed, under a Peace Now poster, with the cat curled up on her lap, quietly writing the names of towns and countries on her collection of matchboxes from dozens of well-known hotels where she has never stayed, San Moritz, St. Tropez, San Marino, Monterrey, San Remo, Lugano.

But what was the Author trying to say?

Rochele Reznik is still sitting on her bed, her hair unplaited, with her legs folded underneath her, white underpants visible under her nightdress, but there is no one to see, the curtains are not at the cleaners', they are tightly drawn against the neighbors. She knows that the Author was definitely talking to her between the lines this evening, that there were more words underneath the words he spoke, and she didn't understand a thing. She will sit here like this for another hour or an hour and a half, not trying to get to sleep but trying to understand what he was saying. What was behind his story about the pharmacist who revealed the secrets of the poisons to him when he was a child? Or about Trotsky's beautiful secret daughter? Or the mother who wanted her son to meet a real live author? Or the uncle who hit a member of the Knesset? Her glance pauses suddenly on the door handle, which for an instant looks as though it is silently moving, as though a hand is tentatively testing to see if she has forgotten to lock up. Is it the staircase rapist?

For an instant she freezes in terror. But then a warm glow drives away the fear and she almost darts to the locked door, to peer through the peephole and open up to him even before he can knock, Come in, I was waiting for you.

But no, she won't do it. She has already experienced enough disappointments and rebuffs, she has too many old scars. So she sits on her bed, staring as if fascinated by the door handle, long after the desperate Author has run headlong down the stairs and bumped his shoulder on the broken door of the meter box.

Until eventually she collapses on her back, exhausted.

The cat comes and lies on her stomach, purring and rubbing the sides of its face against her fingers. They both have their eyes open, watching a moth fluttering around the Peace Now poster with the slogan "Our sons' lives matter more than the patriarchs' graves!"

She draws the sheet over herself and goes on trying to understand, while Joselito continues to watch the moth. The air conditioning hums and blows warm, damp air at her, and she has difficulty sleeping. Occasionally she dozes off briefly, but it is more like fainting than sleeping. During one of these spells she fancies for a moment that she has understood, it was really very simple, but then she wakes, sits up in bed, swats at a mosquito, and once again doesn't know what was expected of her this evening. Why did he ask her to go for that walk after the literary event? What was the meaning of his arm on her shoulder, and then his arm round her waist? And all those stories of his, and the furtive cuddles in that dark backyard? Was she just imagining, a couple of hours ago, that a timid hand tried her door handle, and then that he changed his mind and ran downstairs, before she even had time to make up her mind whether or not to open the door?

Was it him or wasn't it? And why?

No answers come, but she feels sadder and sadder, because only a few moments ago, when she was dozing, she understood it all, completely, and now that she is awake she has forgotten what it was she understood.

The night drags on and on, as if time is standing still.

Joselito is restless: he treads softly all over her body, suddenly nipping her big toe, lies in ambush, his body flattened like a stretched spring, his rippling fur heralding an imminent leap — and then he leaps, scratches the sheet, leaps again, and is suddenly clinging to the curtain with his claws as though he means to rip it to shreds and thus dispose once and for all of her lie to the Author.

So the poet Tsefania Beit-Halachmi, Uncle Bumek, was wrong when he wrote in his book *Rhyming Life and Death* that "You'll always find them side by side: never a groom without a bride." And Rabbi Alter Druyanov was also mistaken in including in his *Book of Jokes and Witticisms* the story about the schlemiel of a circumciser who was late for the circumcision. If you think about it, being late is never funny. It is always irreparable. Actually the angry teacher or deputy head of department Dr. Pessach Yikhat was quite right when he stood up at the end of the evening and declared furiously that one of the roles of literature is to distill from misery and suffering at least a drop of comfort or human kindness. How to put it: to lick our wounds, if not to dress them. At the very least literature should not preen itself on mocking us and picking at our wounds, as modern writers in our days do ad nauseam. All they can write is satire, irony, parody (including self-parody), vicious sarcasm, all steeped in malice. In Dr. Pessach Yikhat's view they should have this fact pointed out to them and they should be reminded of their responsibilities.

Rochele showers in lukewarm water and changes her nightdress. Like the other one, it has two buttons, and she does them both up.

> *An apple falls from the tree.*
> *The tree stands over the apple.*
> *The tree turns yellow. The apple is squashed.*
> *The tree drops yellow leaves.*
> *The leaves cover the wrinkled apple*
> *And a cold wind ruffles them.*
> *The autumn is over and winter is here.*
> *The tree is consumed, the apple rots.*
> *Soon it will come. It will hardly hurt.*

Ten past midnight. The gangster's henchman Mr. Leon and his assistant Shlomo Hougi are sitting under the air conditioner, in front of the TV, in the Hougis' newly done-up living room. Second floor back, two small apartments knocked together to make one big one in a housing development in Yad Eliyahu. Sitting at a table covered with a flowery oilcloth, they are nibbling peanuts, mixed nuts, salted almonds, and sunflower seeds and watching a thriller. (Their wives have been relegated to the kitchen or the other room because this film is not for the faint-hearted.)

Mr. Leon, thickset, bald, his eyes a dirty gray, his nose ridiculously small, like a button lost in the middle of the moon, is remonstrating with his host during a commercial break. Believe me, Hougi, you better take back what you said, look, there's a hundred shekels on the table here says it's not the black guy did it, the dentist killed the three of them, did them in one at a time with that what's-its-name of his, the thing he puts you to sleep with before he pulls your teeth out, that's what he killed 'em with. You'll see for yourself in a minute how wrong you are, you an' your black guy, you're making a big mistake, an' it's gonna cost you a straight hundred, and just be glad we didn't make it five hundred.

Shlomo Hougi hesitates uncomfortably. Well, I'm not saying, maybe it really is the dentist who did them in, not the black, I might have misjudged him, we'll find out soon enough. What I was saying before, it was just my personal opinion of the matter. Nothing more.

A few moments later he adds in a contrite tone: Look, in Judaism it says somewhere, I think it's in Tractate Ta'anit, it says "God has many killers." I heard Rabbi Janah commenting on this, he said maybe it's true that God respected Abel and his offering, but he really preferred Cain. The proof is that Abel died young, before he had time to marry even, so it's a plain fact that the whole human race, including us, I mean the Jewish people, is descended from Cain not from Abel. No offense meant to anyone personally, of course.

Mr. Leon munches a few cashews while he thinks this over, and then he asks: So what? What are you getting at?

And Shlomo Hougi replies sadly: Who? Me? What do I know? There must be loads more about this in Judaism, but personally I'm just on the bottom rung, as they say. I don't know much. Nothing at all, really. Tell me, don't you think it a pity he preferred Cain? Don't you think it would have been better for us if he'd preferred Abel? But he must have had a reason. There's nothing in the whole world that doesn't have a reason. Nothing at all. Even this moth. Even a hair in your soup. Everything there is, without exception, doesn't just testify to itself, it testifies to something else as well. Something big and terrible. In Judaism this is known as "mysteries." Nobody understands them, except the great saints, in the high places among the holy and pure.

Mr. Leon chortles, It's true you're a little cracked, Hougi. More than a little, in fact. Those God-merchants of yours have really messed up your head. What you're saying, it doesn't make much sense. It's not that new either. But since you've fallen into their clutches nothing you say makes any damn sense. Maybe you can explain to me the connection between Cain and Abel and a moth. Or between a hair in the soup and the great saints. You'd be better off shutting your face. That's enough now. Let's watch. The commercials have finished.

Shlomo Hougi thinks this over, and finally, with a guilty, chastened air, he admits almost in a whisper: The truth is, I don't understand either. In fact, I understand less and less. Maybe you're right, the best thing for me to do is to shut up.

.   .   .

Yuval Dahan goes out on the balcony and without turning on the light sprawls in his mother's hammock, ignoring the bats that nest in the ficus tree and the shrill note of the mosquitoes, mentally composing a letter to the Author after the literary evening at the Shunia Shor and the Seven Victims of the Quarry Attack Cultural Center. In his letter the youth will express disgust at the sterile show of erudition displayed by the literary critic in his talk, attempt to express in a few sentences the various emotions he has felt on reading the Author's books, and explain why he senses that the Author is more likely than anyone else in the world to understand his poems, a few of which he makes so bold as to enclose in case the Author can find half an hour to look at them and perhaps even write him a few lines.

For a few minutes he indulges in a fantasy about the Author. After all, the Author probably has sufferings of his own, not as ignoble as mine but just as painful. You can read it between the lines in all his books. Maybe, like me, he has trouble sleeping at night. Perhaps at this very minute he is roaming the streets, all alone, unable to sleep, not wanting to sleep, wandering aimlessly from street to street, struggling like me with the black hole in his chest, and asking himself if there is any point and if there isn't then why on earth?

Soon his wanderings may chance to bring him here, to Reines Street, or rather not chance, because nothing happens by chance. And I'll go out to mail this letter, and at the corner of Gordon Street we'll meet, and we'll both be very surprised at this nocturnal meeting, and he may invite me to keep him company so we can chat on the way, and so we'll talk as we walk, maybe down to the seafront and then left toward Jaffa, and he won't be in a hurry to take his leave, we'll both of us forget what time it is, because he'll discover something in me that reminds him of himself when he was young, and so we'll go on walking through the empty streets toward the Florentin Quarter or maybe to the area around Bialik Street, and we'll go on talking till morning about his books and also a bit about my poems, and also about life and death and all sorts of secret things that I could only talk about to him, not to anyone else, and about suffering in general, because I will be able to explain to him, because he'll be able to understand, he'll understand me at once, even before I've finished explaining he'll have understood everything, and maybe from tonight on there'll be some kind of personal bond between the two of us, we might become like two friends, or like a teacher and a pupil, and so from tonight on everything in my life might be a bit different because of this meeting that's going to happen soon by chance down there, by the mailbox.

Two or three weeks later the Author will reply briefly to Yuval Dahan or Dotan's letter.

I read your poems with interest and found them serious, original, linguistically fresh, but first of all you must learn to curb your excess of emotion and write with more distance. As if you the person writing the poems and you the suffering young man are two different people, and as though the former observes the latter coolly, distantly, even with a measure of amusement. Maybe you should try writing as though the two of you were separated by a hundred years, that is as though there were a gap of a century between the young man in the poem and the poet, between the pain he feels and the time you are writing.

P.S. You are not quite right in your harsh criticism of the lecturer, Bar-Orian. True, he is apparently not a very nice man, and I was sorry to learn that at the end of the evening he dismissed you rather rudely, but it is not correct to say of him that "he is a stranger to life": for some years he has been living alone in a ground-floor apartment in Adam Ha-Cohen Street, he has been widowed twice, he teaches in the Kibbutz College, you probably didn't know that his only daughter Aya walked out on him when she was only sixteen and a half, changed her name to Jocelyn, hung around in New York for two years, posed nude for magazines, then got religion and married a settler from Elon Moreh, and now, for the past two to three weeks, Mr. Bar-Orian has been torturing himself to decide whether to keep to his boycott or to close his eyes to his conscience and his principles and agree, just this once, and certainly not to create a precedent, to cross the Green Line into the Occupied Territories to visit his settler daughter and hold his baby settler grandson in his arms for the first time.

•   •   •

Or take Ovadya Hazzam, for example, Hazzam from Isratex, the man who won the lottery, got divorced, had a
wild time, lent money left and right to all comers, cruised
around town in a blue Buick, contributed to collections for
new Torah scrolls, financed a pirate religious radio station
out of his own pocket, spent money like water on good
causes and also on divorcees from Russia, bought land in
the Territories, rushed into politics, moved house six times
in two years, married his elder son to Lucy, runner-up in
the Queen of the Waves contest, Yitzhak Shamir and Shimon Peres both attended the glittering wedding, the hun-
dreds of guests kissed him and he, in a blue silk suit with a
triangle of white handkerchief in his breast pocket, kissed
and hugged every one of them, men and women, members
of the Knesset, land dealers, artists, journalists, he hugged
and kissed the lot of them, with tears of emotion, joked
and laughed, made them all taste — just taste — another
piece of cake, have another drink, and now he is lying on
a sweaty bed in the damp darkness of the hospital ward,
between two other dying men, his bedclothes soaked in
urine, with bits of dried blood clinging to his nostrils and
the corners of his mouth, with a painful wheezing sound
he breathes through an oxygen mask that covers his nose
and mouth, and as his chest rises and falls he half remembers in his morphine-induced haze lots of hands stroking
his head, shoulders, and chest, a woman or women weeping, and closing his eyes he can suddenly see the Sources
of the Jordan: a sunbathed landscape with choirs of birds

and a shady eucalyptus grove between two streams. The trees are massive, and almost belong to the realm of the inanimate. The place is far away and peaceful. Apart from the twittering of the birds and the occasional sound of the breeze high up in the trees, the silence is intense. An unseen bee is buzzing in the heart of the sunlight. And two birds reply. Some time ago there was heavy rain all over Galilee with thunder and high winds. Now all is calm. The air is brilliant, polished, and the view as far as the mountain slopes is bathed in limpid light. There are ripples on the surface of the two streams. Every now and again a curl of foam dances on the water, or a shoal of fish stirs under the surface like a silent caress. The slowly falling leaves rustle constantly in the twilight under the oxygen mask, and there is an occasional grunting sound or a stifled guttural scraping like a car slithering on thick gravel, that now pierces the sleep of Ricky the waitress and causes her to utter a couple of frightened sobs and chase away with a sleepy hand some evil shadow that bends over her and presses down on her sheet in the dark. Crafty, patient and kindly, Berl Katznelson, still looking down from his picture at the cultural center, knew how to pull off a discreet coup by rather devious means: this is a bad business, all of it here, ridiculous and terrible.

It is still warm and humid inside, and thick darkness outside. The Author lights a last cigarette and soon he will lie down to sleep. Sounds of four o'clock in the morning come to him through the window: the swish of a sprinkler on the lawn, broken cries of alarm from a parked car that can no longer bear its loneliness, the low weeping of a man in the next-door apartment, on the other side of the wall, the shriek of a nightbird nearby that can perhaps already see what is hidden from you and me. Tell me, have you ever heard the name of Tsefania Beit-Halachmi? *Rhyming Life and Death*? No? He was a minor poet whose verses were once quite well known here but over the years they have been forgotten. The poet who was wrong about that groom and bride, side by side. And now, the nightbird has stopped its shrieking, and in the evening paper that was waiting for me by my bed I read that in the early hours of yesterday morning, in Raanana, at the age of ninety-seven, the poet died in his sleep of heart failure. Once in a while it is worth turning on the light to clarify what is going on. Tomorrow will be warm and humid, too. And, in fact, tomorrow is today.

The Characters

The Author

Ricky: a waitress. Once she was in love with Charlie, the reserve goalkeeper of Bnei-Yehuda football team, who affectionately referred to her as Gogog.

Charlie: the reserve goalkeeper of Bnei-Yehuda football team. Had a good time in Eilat with both Ricky and Lucy. Now owns a factory that manufactures solar water heaters in Holon and even exports them to Cyprus.

Lucy: runner-up in the Queen of the Waves contest. She also had a good time in Eilat with Charlie. In the end she had a glittering wedding to the son of Ovadya Hazzam from Isratex.

Mr. Leon: gangster's henchman. Thickset and bossy.

Shlomo Hougi: Mr. Leon's assistant. Understands less and less.

Ovadya Hazzam: used to work for Isratex. Had a blue Buick. Used to drive around with various close friends, immigrants from Russia. Now he is in the hospital with cancer, and no one comes to empty his catheter bag.

Ovadya Hazzam's son: married Lucy, runner-up in the
Queen of the Waves contest. Yitzhak Shamir and Shimon Peres came to the wedding.

Shunia Shor and the Seven Victims of the Quarry Attack:
Shunia Shor was a mechanic, ideologue and composer
of folk songs. Was killed in 1937, with seven other
workers at the Tel Hazon quarry, by Arab youths who
had decided to drive the Jews out of the country. The
community center where the Author meets his readers
was named after Shunia Shor and the seven victims of
the quarry attack.

Yerucham Shdemati: cultural administrator. Runs the
Shunia Shor and the Seven Victims of the Quarry Attack Cultural Center. Likes to lick the gummed side
of postage stamps with the whole of his tongue. Not a
well man.

Rabbi Alter Druyanov: author of *The Book of Jokes and
Witticisms*.

Rochele Reznik: professional reader, who reads aloud the
words of famous writers. Collects matchboxes from famous hotels round the world.

Yakir Bar-Orian (Zhitomirski): literary critic. Widower.
His only daughter is married to a famous settler in
Elon Moreh settlement.

Tsefania Beit-Halachmi: poet. His real name, so far as I
know, is Avraham (Bumek) Schuldenfrei. Author of
Rhyming Life and Death. Wrong about one thing.

Berl Katznelson: in the picture hanging on the wall at the
cultural center he looks crafty and kindly.

Miriam Nehorait: culture lover. Makes sticky fruit compote. Children in her neighborhood call her Mira the Horror behind her back.

Yechiel Nehorai: husband of Miriam Nehorait. Was run over nine years ago when he was a Zionist emissary in Montevideo.

Yuval Dahan/Dotan: very young poet. Not happy.

Dr. Pessach Yikhat: veteran teacher or deputy head of a regional educational department. Takes a dim view of current trends in literature.

Joselito: Rochele Reznik's cat. Jealous. Can tell the time. And makes her feel guilty.

Uncle Osya: piano tuner. House painter. Once, many years ago, forgot the Author (who was still a child at the time) at the Pogrebinsky Brothers' pharmacy. Some say that for a year or two he hid the niece of Leon Trotsky in his basement apartment on Brenner Street.

Shmuel Mikunis: member of the Knesset (Israel Communist Party). Once Uncle Osya nearly hit him, but later, when they both fell ill of the same disease in the same year, they became friends and even took care of each other.

Madame Pogrebinskaya (from the Pogrebinsky Brothers' pharmacy): dragged the Author, who was still a child at the time, into a dark back room and showed him something and even explained in a whisper.

Short woman with glasses and a green-and-white-striped pantsuit: mother of Sagiv, who has never seen a real live writer close up, which is why it is very important for him to see the Author close up. Once spoke to Mrs. Lea Goldberg at the grocer's.

Sagiv: almost nine. Does not speak. Has no wish at all to see a writer, only wants to break free and run away, but his mother holds him very tightly by the arm, just above the elbow.

Lisaveta Kunitsin: neighbor. Optician. Once happened to peep and see something.

Lisaveta Shuminer: mother of Yerucham Shdemati. Died in Kharkov sixty-six years ago. Dreamed of being a famous singer. Her seventy-two-year-old son still sometimes dreams of her.

Aya (Jocelyn): daughter of Yakir Bar-Orian. Was once photographed in the nude in New York and is now married to a famous settler in Elon Moreh settlement.

Baby: son of the settler and Aya, grandson of Yakir Bar-Orian.

Arnold Bartok: petty party hack, gaunt and bespectacled. Sacked from the local branch and later fired from his part-time job sorting parcels in a private courier company. Interested in eternal life. Apparently only came to the literary event to mock the Author.

Ophelia: invalid mother of Arnold Bartok. Eighty-six. Paralyzed from the waist down. Dependent on a chamber pot. Sleeps on the same mattress as her sixty-year-old son and insists on calling him Araleh, to annoy him, even though his name is Arnold and he's already told her so a thousand times.

Thickset night watchman: stands and pisses.

Photographer from the days of sepia photographs: arranges everybody and tells them when to smile and when not to move please.

Miriam Nehorait's cat: refused to listen to the photographer and moved when the picture was being taken, so came out with three or four tails.

Miriam Nehorait's two married sons: gynecologists in New York. One of them is married to Lisaveta Kunitsin's daughter.

Yerucham Shdemati's brother's granddaughter: fourteen and a half years old, and they still ask her childish riddles.

Yerucham Shdemati's doctor brother: told Yerucham Shdemati that his chances of recovery from the blood disease he is suffering from are remote.

Wives of Mr. Leon and Shlomo Hougi, respectively: relegated to the kitchen because the film on TV is not for them.

ARAD, 2006